William Clark Russell

**An ocean tragedy**

William Clark Russell

**An ocean tragedy**

ISBN/EAN: 9783337046194

Printed in Europe, USA, Canada, Australia, Japan

Cover: Foto ©Andreas Hilbeck / pixelio.de

More available books at **www.hansebooks.com**

BY

W. CLARK RUSSELL

AUTHOR OF 'THE FROZEN PIRATE' 'THE WRECK OF THE GROSVENOR'
'A BOOK FOR THE HAMMOCK' 'THE ROMANCE OF
JENNY HARLOWE' ETC.

IN THREE VOLUMES

VOL. II.

London

CHATTO & WINDUS, PICCADILLY

1890

PRINTED BY
SPOTTISWOODE AND CO., NEW-STREET SQUARE
LONDON

# CONTENTS

OF

## THE SECOND VOLUME

# AN OCEAN TRAGEDY.

## CHAPTER XIV.

### MUFFIN GOES FORWARD.

I ROSE next morning shortly after seven, bathed and went to the cabin for a cup of coffee. I could see through the skylight that it was a fine day. The air showed a bright blue against the glass, and a rich tremble of sunlight was on the thick crystal of every weather porthole, the glory rippling with the reflective throbbing and running of the sea, as it broke upon the polished panels abreast or flashed in the confronting mirrors. The ocean was quiet too; the heave of the yacht was gentle, though the heel of her gave assurance of a breeze of wind. The two stewards were busy in the cabin. I knew that Finn would have the forenoon watch, since Crimp had had charge from eight to midnight, and I called to the head steward to know if the captain was about.

'Not yet, sir, I believe.'

'Take my compliments to him, and say I should like to see him at once, if possible—here, in the cabin, I mean.'

Whilst I waited, Muffin, hearing my voice, came from his berth. I watched him out of the corner of my eyes; he slowly advanced in a sort of writhing way, making many grimaces as he approached, as if in the throes of rehearsing a speech, and presently stood before me, first casting a look at the second steward who was polishing a looking-glass, and then clasping his hands before him and hanging his head.

'Mr. Monson, I 'umbly ask your pardon, sir. May I beg that out of your kind 'art you will overlook my doings last night? Sir, I do not find myself partial to the hocean, and my desire is to return 'ome, sir. I meant no 'arm. I would not wrong an 'air of Sir Wilfrid's 'ed. My five years' character from the Right Honourable the Lord Sandown speaks to my morals, sir. I am sincerely remorseful, Mr. Monson, and trust to be made 'appy by your forgiving me, sir.'

I listened to what he had to say, and then exclaimed, 'My forgiveness has nothing to do with the matter. You are not a person fit to wait upon Sir Wilfrid Monson, and—but I shall have something to tell you a little later on. Meanwhile, you can go.'

He said unctuously, 'Am I to take Sir Wilfrid his 'ot water as usual, sir?'

'Yes,' I said, 'continue to wait on him.'

He plucked up at this and withdrew with an ill-dissembled smirk upon his countenance. Presently Captain Finn came trundling down the cabin steps, cap in hand, his long face bright with recent cleansing, and full of expectation. I asked him to sit, and then, without a word of preface, I bluntly told him about the 'warnings' my cousin had received for two nights running, and how last night my suspicion, in some unaccountable way, having been aroused, I entered the baronet's berth and found Muffin painting the sentence in a vermin-killing composition of phosphorus. Finn whistled.

'The weasel!' he cried; 'how is he to be punished for this? Will ye have him ducked from the yard-arm, or seized up aloft, or played on with the hose for spells of half-an-hour, or whipped up for a grease-down job that 'll last him nigh a day? Say the word, sir. I feel to want the handling of a chap whose veins look to run slush, to judge by his colour and the lay of his hair.'

'No,' said I, 'no need to deal with him as

you suggest. But he must be turned out of this end of the vessel and sent into the forecastle. Before we decide, however, can you make use of him?'

'Ay can I. Leave him to me, your honour,' said Finn, grinning. 'I'll make a man of him.'

'Steward,' I called, 'send Muffin to me.'

The valet arrived, looking hard at Finn. I made some excuse to get the stewards out of the cabin, and then said, 'Now, Muffin, attend. You are at once to decide whether you will go forward amongst the men, live with them in the forecastle and do such work as Captain Finn appoints, or whether Sir Wilfrid shall be told of last night's business that he may deal with you as he thinks proper.'

Finn gazed at him with a frown and a cheek purpled by indignation and contempt. The fellow fixed his dead black eye on me, and said, 'I would rather go 'ome, sir.'

'I dessay you would!' burst out Finn. 'How will 'ee travel? By locomotive or post-chay? By my grandmother's bones! if one of my men had played such a trick on me as you've played on your master, I'd spreadeagle him with these here hands if he was as tall as my mainmast, and lay on till there wasn't a rag of flesh left to tickle.'

I motioned silence with an indication with my head in the direction of Sir Wilfrid's berth.

'Take your choice, and be sharp about it,' said I, turning hotly upon Muffin, whose very sleekness at such a time was a kind of insolence in him somehow; 'either decide to be dealt with by Sir Wilfrid, who probably will shoot you for what you have done, or go to him after he has risen, tell him that you have made up your mind to discontinue your services as a valet, and that you have requested Captain Finn to place you upon the articles as a boy.'

'Ay, as a boy,' echoed Finn in a half-suppressed note of storm, and fetching his leg a mighty thump with his clenched fist.

Muffin's left leg fell away, he clasped his hands in a posture of prayer upon his shirt-front, and, after looking in a weeping way from Finn to me, and from me to Finn, he said, snuffling as he spoke, 'Gentlemen, give me an 'arf hour to think it over, I beg of you.'

I pulled out my watch. 'I must have your decision by eight o'clock,' said I. 'See to it. If you do not decide for yourself, I shall choose for you, and give my cousin the whole truth; though for your sake,' I added, with a menacing look at him, 'as well as for his, I am very desirous indeed that he should remain ignorant of your conduct. Go!'

I sat talking with Finn. His indignation increased upon him as we spoke of Muffin's behaviour.

'It was enough to drive his honour clean mad, sir,' he exclaimed. 'Why, though there's little I believes in outside what my senses tells me of, I allow I should feel like jumping overboard if so be on putting out the light I found a piece of adwice wrote upon the dark in letters of fire. But I'll work his old iron up for that job. There's something leagues out of the ordinary in that there slush-made cove, sir. 'Taint that I hobjects to a man who never looks me in the eye. But there's something in the appearance of that there Muffin which makes me think that if he could pull his heart out of his breast he'd find it like a piece of rotten ship's bread, full of weevils and holes.'

'The man is pining for the shore,' said I. 'The fellow thought to work upon the weak side of my cousin's intellect. He meant no more, I believe, than to frighten Sir Wilfrid into returning. He remains a very good valet all the same, though we must have him out of this. He will not be the only servant in the world who has procured his or her ends by working on the master's or mistress's fears.'

'Well, I suppose not, sir,' said Finn; 'taking men-servants all round they're a bad lot. I never yet see one, specially if he wore big calves and had got white hair, but that I felt a longing to have him at sea for a month. By the way, sir, talking of this here Muffin's mystifying of his honour, what d'ye think, Mr. Monson, sir? Blowed if old Crimp, who I shouldn't ha' credited with a single idea outside the tar bucket, hain't gone and fallen superstitious! When I relieved him at midnight he up and spins a long twister about you and him having heard a woice holloing a curse upon this yacht away out on the starboard quarter somewhere.'

He broke into a low, deep sea laugh which he endeavoured to check by clapping his hand to his mouth.

'We heard something,' said I, 'that sounded like a voice, and we made out the noise to signify the same thing. It may have been a bird, or some mysterious fish come up to breathe, or some singular sound produced by the yacht herself. No matter what,—I have dismissed it from my mind.'

'Poor old Jacob!' he continued, smothering another laugh; 'why, sir, he'd actually thought hisself into a clam when I went on deck and said he reckoned this part of the hocean much colder than the coast o' Greenland. Jacob's being so werry commonplace is the reason of my thinking nothen of the yarn. Had he even a little bit more mind than belongs to him I'd be willing to allow his story was a queer one; but he's so empty of any sort o' intellects short of the ones that he needs to enable him to keep a look-out and attend to the navigation of the craft, that his werry hollowness touches 'tother extreme of a brain chock ablock with fantastical ideas; by which I mean that I'd as lief attend to a madman's notion of a strange woice as to Jacob's. Not but that he ain't as trustworthy, practical a sailor as I could wish to have by my side if I ever found myself in a quandary.'

I cast my eye at the clock under the skylight. As I did so, Muffin came sliding towards us with exactly the same sort of gait and countenance you would expect in a well-practised funeral mute. He approached close before speaking, and postured in front of me, preserving a respectful silence, whilst he kept his eyes fastened on the deck.

'Well?' said I.

'I've been considering the matter, sir, and beg to state that I've made up my mind.'

'Well?' I repeated.

'It might 'urt Sir Wilfrid's feelings, gentlemen, if you, Mr. Monson, sir, explained away the cause of what had alarmed him, and I'll not deny that as his strength of mind isn't such as to give him control over his passions, sir, I should go in fear. Which being so, I'm willing to tell him that I desire to discontinue my services as valet, and should be glad to become what I've 'eard Captain Finn describe as an 'and until such times as we fall in with a ship that may be willing to carry me 'ome. To which, Mr. Monson, sir, and you, Capt'n Finn, I trust, gentlemen, both, you'll have no objection.'

I preserved my gravity with difficulty.

'Very well,' said I, witnessing in the vague indeterminable twinkle of the unpolished jet of his eye that he detected in me the mirth I flattered myself I had concealed; 'after breakfast you will convey your resolution to Sir Wilfrid, of course taking care to insist if he should object, for after what has happened your connection with him must *cease*.'

'As you wish, sir,' he exclaimed, giving me a bow with the whole spine of him; 'but, gentlemen, I should like to state that whatever may be the work Captain Finn puts me to I would rather do it as an 'and than as a boy.'

I felt a bit sorry for the poor devil. It seemed to me that he had accepted his alternative with some pluck.

'A boy is the next grade to ordinary seaman,' said I; 'you will be a hand just the same.'

'What can you do?' exclaimed Finn, running his eye over the figure of the man with an expression that was not one of quite unmixed contempt. 'Can 'ee go aloft?'

The fellow clasped his hands and turned up the whites of his eyes. 'Not to save my precious soul, sir.'

'You can row,' said I.

'I'll feather an oar agin any Thames waterman,' exclaimed Muffin.

'Enough has been said,' I exclaimed, rising. 'The stewards wait to lay the cloth for breakfast,' and so saying, I mounted on deck, followed by the captain, who, after I had exchanged a few words with him, went forward to break his fast before relieving old Crimp.

There was a large full-rigged ship on the weather beam. We were slowly passing her. She was an East Indiaman, I think, of a frigate-like stateliness, with her white band and black ports, and her spacious rounds of canvas tapering in spires to the delicate gossamer of the topmost cloths. The red ensign was waving at her peak as it was at ours, but then she was from England as we were, and had no more news to give us than we her. The bosoms of her canvas arched towards us with the rigging under each curve fine as wire against the sky that sloped to the horizon white and blinding as irradiated steel with the eastern gushing of glory there. There was just swell enough to heave a little space of her coppered forefoot out of the glittering brine that came brimming to her in a liquid blue light, and the rhythmic flash of the metal over the curl of snow at the stem gave an inexpressible grace to the dignity and majesty of the lofty and swelling fabric of cream-coloured cloths, each softened by an airy pinion of shadow at its lee clew. 'Twas wonderful the magic that ship had to vitalise and to subdue to human sympathy the brilliant, weltering wilderness of the morning ocean. She carried the thoughts away to the Thames and to Gravesend, to leave-takings and weeping women and the coming and going of boats, to the hurricane note of the Jacks getting the anchor, to the waving of handkerchiefs up on the poop, to the smell of hay for the live-stock, the gabble of poultry, the cries of children, the loud calls of officers, the ceaseless movements of passengers, stewards, friends, sailors, crowding and elbowing, talking, shaking hands and crying upon the main deck. All this, I say, she made one think of, with a fancy, too, of the rushing Hooghley, a burning atmosphere sickly with the smell of the incense of the hubble-bubble, with a flavour of hot curry about, a dead black body gliding slowly past, the lip, lip, of the rushing stream against the ship's bow and seething to the gang-way ladder, the fiery cabins o' nights vibratory with the horns of the mosquitoes like a distant concert of Jew's harps mingling with the distant unearthly wail of the jackal. Pooh! 'twas a fit of imagination for its torrid atmosphere and Asiatic smells to make one mechanically mop the brow with one's handkerchief. Why, far off as that Indiaman was the clear cool wind seemed to breeze down *hot* from her with an odour of bamboo and cocoanut rope, and chafing gear wrought from the jungle with strange aromas of oils along with the shriek of the paroquet and the hoarse musings of the macaw. I turned to surly old Jacob.

'Good-morning, Mr. Crimp.'

'Marning.'

'Fine ship out yonder.'

'Well, I've seen uglier vessels.'

I approached him close. 'Heard any more voices, Mr. Crimp?'

'No,' he answered, thrusting his fingers into the door-mat of oakum upon his throat, 'and I don't want to.'

'I advised you to keep your counsel,' said I, 'but I find that you have spoken to Captain Finn.'

'Who wouldn't? My mind ain't a demijean, smother me! It's not big enough to hold the likes of last night's job. Told the capt'n? 'Course I did.'

I saw that he was a mule of a man, and not proper to reason with. I said with an air of indifference, 'Have you thought the thing over? Was it a bird, as I said at the time, or a noise breaking out perhaps from the inside of the yacht, and by deception of the hearing sounding in syllables apparently away out upon the sea?'

He eyed me dully, and after a stupid, staring pause, exclaimed, 'I wish *you* hadn't heard it.'

'Why?'

'Why? 'Cause then I might ha' believed it was *my* fancy; but as I says to the capt'n, two collected intellects ain't going to get the same meaning out o' what's got no sense. I hope that this here trip may turn out all right, that's all. I've been a going to sea now for thirty year, but smite me if ever I was in a wessel afore that was damned in the first watch by a woice a sounding out of the blackness with nothen for it to come from.'

The breakfast bell now rang, and I went below not a little surprised by this exhibition of superstitious alarm in so sour and matter-of-fact a seaman as Jacob Crimp. For my part, though I admit the thing greatly puzzled me, it was only as some conjuring trick might. Perhaps with old Crimp I should have been better satisfied had but one of us heard the voice; or, presuming us both to have caught the sound, had we each made a different sentence of it. *There* lay the real oddness of the incident, but as to supposing there was anything supernatural in it, I should have needed the brains of my cousin, who could interpret Muffin's stale and vulgar trick into a solemn injunction, perhaps from heaven, to think so.

Wilfrid joined us at breakfast; he made a good meal, and was easy in his spirits. I asked him if he had been troubled with any more warnings. He answered no, nothing whatever had occurred to disturb him. He had slept soundly, and had not passed so good a night for days and days. 'But,' said he with a glance round the cabin, for the valet had been hanging about, though he did not station himself behind his master's chair as heretofore, 'if I were ashore

I should be prepared for another kind of warning, I mean a warning from Muffin, if I may judge by his face and manner. Something is wrong with the fellow.'

'You once suspected his sanity,' said I, smiling. 'Upon my word I cannot persuade myself that such a dial plate as his covers sound clockwork. He strikes wrongly, I'm sure. He don't keep true time, Wilf.'

'Do you think so really?' he exclaimed with some anxiety.

'Do you believe Muffin to be perfectly sound, Miss Jennings?' said I, giving her a significant glance.

'I should be very sorry to trust him,' she answered with a spirited gaze at Wilfrid.

The subject dropped; our conversation went to the Indiaman that lay for a little, whilst we sat at the breakfast table, framed in the cabin port-hole abreast of us, coming and going with the light reel of the yacht, but whenever set for a moment then the most dainty and lovely image imaginable, like to some small choice wondrous carving in mother-of-pearl of a ship, shot with many subtle complexions of light as though you viewed her through a rainbow of fairy-like tenuity. Then, having talked of her, we passed on to our voyage, till on a sudden a fit of sullenness fell upon

Wilfrid, and he became moody; but, happily, I had by this time finished my breakfast, and as I had no notion of an argument, nor of courting one of his hot, reproachful, vexing speeches touching his own anguish and my coldness, I left the table, telling Miss Jennings that she would find her chair, rugs, and novel ready for her on deck when she should be pleased to join me.

She arrived alone in about half-an-hour. There was something so fragrant in her presence, so flower-like in her aspect, that she could not approach you but that it was as though she brought a nosegay with her whose perfume had a sweetness for every sense of the body. We had not been long together, yet already I might have guessed what had happened with me by noticing in myself the impatience with which I desired her company, the repeated glances I would send at the companion hatch if I expected her on deck, the very comfortable feeling of satisfaction, the emotion indeed of quiet delight that possessed me when I had her snug by my side in her chair, with no one to break in upon us but Wilfrid, who troubled us very little in this way. I remember this morning when I took the novel off her lap to see what progress she had made in it, thinking, as my glance went in a smile from the mark in the middle of chapter the third to her eyes, in which lay a delicate light of laughter, that before long we should be having the weather of the tropics, the radiant ivory of the equinoctial moon, the dew-laden stillness of the equatorial calm, and that there might come night after night of oceanic repose for us to enjoy—and enjoy alone; but I almost started to the fancy, for it was a sort of secret recantation, a quiet confession of my heart to my reason that though to be sure this voyage was to be viewed as a goose-chase, I was beginning to feel willing that it should not be so brief as I was quite lately trusting it would prove. No wonder the old poets represented love as a kind of madness, seeing that a man who suffers from this disorder will, like a madman, experience twenty different moods in an hour.

'You do not appear to find the dukes and earls of this star-and-garter novel very engaging company,' said I, placing the book in her lap again.

'It is a good sort of novel to dream over,' said she; 'the moment I look at it I find my mind thinking of something else.'

'A pity Wilfrid cannot read,' said I, 'but his mind, like the poet's eye, glances too much. There are two unfailing tests of brain power: the appreciation of humour and the capacity of concentration.'

'Might not a very clever man laugh at a very silly joke?' she asked.

'Yes, but his laugh will be of a different sort from a stupid fellow's at the same joke. Where did you leave Wilfrid?'

'In the cabin. Muffin came up to me just now, apparently on his way to his master, and begged me in a most strange, suppliant hollow way to implore you not to allow Sir Wilfrid to suspect that the handwriting was a trick; "for," said the man, "if he gets that notion into his head he will suspect me, and then, miss," he said, "the baronet might take my life, for if he's scarcely responsible for what he does when he's in a good temper, what would he not be capable of when he's in a dreadful passion?" This was in effect what he said. His language and manner are not to be imitated. I told him very coldly that neither of us was likely to tell Sir Wilfrid, not because we should not be very pleased to see him punished by his master as he deserved, even though it came to his shooting him,' she exclaimed, lifting her eyes to mine with roguish enjoyment of Muffin's terror, 'but because we were anxious that Sir Wilfrid should be spared the humiliation of the discovery.'

'Muffin will be out of this end of the ship before noon,' said I.

'What have you arranged?'

'His name will be entered in the articles as a boy, that is as a sailor below the grade of an ordinary seaman.'

'Is he to work as a sailor?'

'Finn will try him.'

'The poor wretch!' she cried, looking aloft; 'have you ever observed his feet? Such a man as that cannot climb.'

'They'll put him to deck work,' said I; 'scrubbing, polishing, scraping, painting.' She fell silent with her gaze upon the open book. Presently she sent a slow, thoughtful look along the sea and sighed.

'Mr. Monson, I wonder if we shall fall in with the "Shark"?'

I shook my head.

'But why not?' she exclaimed with a pretty pettishness.

'She might be yonder at this moment,' said I pointing to the light-blue horizon that lined like an edging of glass the sky upon our starboard beam. 'Who is to tell? Our field is too big for such a chase.'

'We shall find them at Table Bay then,' she said defiantly.

'Or rather let us hope that they will find us there. But suppose we pick the "Shark" up; suppose we are lying in Table Bay when she arrives. What is to happen? What end is to be served? On my honour, if Lady Monson were my wife——' I snapped my fingers.

'You are cold-hearted.'

'I am practical.'

'You would not extend your hand to lift up one who has fallen.'

'Do not put it so. The girl I marry will, of course, be an angel.' Her lips twitched to a smile. 'If she expands her wings and flies away from me, am I to pick up a blunderbuss with the notion of potting her as she makes sail? No, let her go. She is indeed still an angel, but a bad angel. A bad angel is of no use to a man She poisons his heart, she addles his brains, she renders his sleep loathsome with nightmares, she buries a stiletto in the vitalest part of his honour. *Follow* her, forsooth! I could be eloquent,' said I with a young man's confident laugh, 'but I must remember that I am talking to Laura Jennings.'

We were interrupted by Wilfrid. He came slowly forking up through the hatch in his long-limbed way, and approached us with excitement in his manner.

'Mad!' he cried with a look over his shoulder. 'Mad, as you say. by George! you were both right, and I'm deuced glad to have made the discovery. Why, here was this fellow, d'ye see, Charles, hanging about me at all hours of the day, free to enter my room at any time when I might be in bed and sound asleep. Confoundedly odd though.'

'Are you talking of Muffin?' said I.

'Ay, of Muffin to be sure.'

'He's not gone mad, I hope?'

'I think so, anyway,' he answered with a wise nod that was made affecting to me by the tremble in his lids, and the childish assumption of shrewdness and knowingness you found in his eyes and the look of his face.

'What has he done?' asked Miss Jennings, playing with the leaves of the volume on her knee.

'Why, he just now came to my cabin,' answered my cousin, sending a glance at the skylight, 'and told me that he was weary of his duties as a valet, and desired to be at once released. I said to him, "What do you mean? We're at sea, man. This is not a house that you can walk out from!" He answered he knew that. He desired to go into the forecastle and work as a sailor—as a sailor! Figure Muffin astride of a lee yardarm in a gale of wind.' He broke into one of his short roars of laughter, but immediately grew grave, and proceeded: 'There was a tone of insolence in the fellow that struck me. It might have been because he had made up his mind, expected that I should refuse, and had come resolved to bounce, even to offensively bounce me into consenting. Besides, too, there was an expression in his eye which satisfied me that yours and Laura's suspicions were sound—were sound. But I did not need to witness any physical symptom of mental derangement. Enough surely that this sleek, obsequious, ghostly though somewhat gouty rascal, whom I cannot imagine fit for any post in the world but that of valet, should throw up his comfortable berth with us in the cabin to become what he calls "an 'and." Ha! ha! ha!' His vast, odd shout of laughter rang through the yacht from end to end.

'Of course,' said I, 'you told him to go forward.'

'Oh, certainly. I should not love to have a lunatic waiting upon me. Why, damme, there are times when I have let that fellow shave me. But—I say, Charles—Muffin as an 'and, eh?'

He turned on his heel, shaking with laughter, and walked up to Finn, to whom I heard him tell the whole story, though repeatedly interrupting himself with a jerky, noisy shout of merriment. He asked the skipper what work he could put Muffin to, and Finn rumbled out a long answer, but they stood at too great a distance to enable me to catch all that was said. Presently Finn put his head into the companion hatchway and called. After a little Muffin emerged. Wilfrid recoiled when he saw the man, turned his back upon him, and stepped hastily right aft past the wheel. I whispered to Miss Jennings, 'Did you mark that? Each will go in terror of the other now, I suppose; Wilfrid because he thinks Muffin mad, and Muffin because he thinks that Wilfrid, should he get to hear the truth, will shoot him.'

'This way, my lad,' cried Finn in a Cape-Horn voice, and a half smile that twisted the hole in the middle of his long visage till it looked like the mouth of a plaice. They both went forward and disappeared. The sailors who were at work about the deck stared hard at Muffin as he passed them, shrewdly guessing that something unusual had happened, and not a little astonished to observe the captain conducting him between decks to the mariners' parlour. Soon the skipper came up, and called to a large, burly, heavily-whiskered man, who, as I had gathered, was a sort of acting boatswain, though I believe he had not signed in that capacity, but had been appointed by Finn to oversee the crew as being the most experienced sailor on board. The skipper talked with him, and the heavily-whiskered man nodded vehemently with a broad smile that compressed his face into a thousand wrinkles, under the rippling of which his little eyes seemed to founder altogether. Then Finn came aft, and Wilfrid and he fell to pacing the deck.

Miss Jennings read; I smoked occasionally, giving her an excuse to leave her book by asking a question, or uttering some commonplace remark. I was lying back in my easy, lounging deck-chair, with my eyes sleepily following the languid sweep of the maintopmast-head, where the truck showed like a circle of hoar frost against the airy blue that floated in its soft, cool bright tint to the edges of the sails whose brilliant whiteness seemed to overflow the bolt ropes and frame them with a narrow band of pearl-coloured film, when Miss Jennings suddenly exclaimed, 'Oh, Mr. Monson, do look!'

I started, and, following the direction of her gaze, spied Muffin standing near the galley rigged out as a sailor. There may have been a slop-chest on board—I cannot tell; perhaps Finn had borrowed the clothes for the fellow from one of the seamen; anyway there stood Muffin, divested of his genteel frock coat, his gentlemanly cravat and black cloth unmentionables, and equipped in a sailor's jacket of that period, a coarse coloured shirt, rough duck or canvas breeches, whose bell-shaped extremities entirely concealed his gouty ankles. His head was protected by a nautical straw hat, somewhat battered, with one long ribbon floating down his back, under the brim of which his yellow face showed with the primrose tincture of the Chinaman, whilst his dead black eyes, gazing languishingly our way, looked the deader and the blacker for the plaster-like streak of hair that lay along his brow as though one of the Jacks had scored a line there with a brush steeped in liquid pitch.

'Heavens, what an actor the fellow would make!' said I, the laugh that seemed to have risen to my throat lying checked there by wonder and even admiration of the astonishing figure the man cut in his new attire. The burly, heavily-whiskered salt rolled up to him. What Muffin said I could not hear, but there was the air of a respectful bow in the posture of his odd form, and my ear easily imagined the oily tone of his replies to the huge sailor. They crossed to the other side of the deck out of sight.

Shortly afterwards I left my seat to join Wilfrid, and then the first object that I beheld on the port side of the vessel was Muffin washing the side of the galley with a bucket of water at his feet and the heavily-whiskered man looking on. Well, thought I, rounding on my heel with a laugh, 'twill make home the sweeter to him when he gets there, and meanwhile Wilfrid will be free from all further phosphoric visitations.

# CHAPTER XV.

## I BOARD A WRECK.

The time slipped by. Life is monotonous at sea, and, though the days seem to have speeded quickly past when one looks back, they appear to be crawling along on all-fours when one looks ahead. We sighted nothing that carried the least resemblance to the vessel we were in chase of. Within a week we spoke two ships, both Englishmen, one a fine tall black clipper craft from Sydney, New South Wales, full of Colonials bound to the old country for a cruise amongst the sights there; the other a little north-country brig laden down to her chain plates in charge of the very tallest man I ever saw in my life, this side I mean of the giants who go on show, with a roaring voice that smote the ear like the blast of a discharged piece; but neither vessel gave us any news of the 'Shark,' no craft of the kind had been sighted or heard of by either of them.

It was as I expected. For my part the adventure remained a most ridiculous undertaking, and never more so than when I thought of the speck a ship made in the vast blue eye of the wide ocean. We fell in with some handsome breezes for travelling, several of which drove us through it in thunder with a hill of foam on either quarter and an acre of creaming white spreading under the chaste golden beauty the yacht carried on her stem-head. The wind flashed blue into the violet hollows of the canvas, the curves of whose round breasts shone out past the shadowings to the sun, and rang splitting upon the iron taut rigging of the driven craft with joyous hunting-notes in its echoings as though the chase were in view and there were spirits in the air hallooing us into a madder speeding.

Wilfrid and Finn and I hung over the chart, calculating with sober faces, finding our position to be there and then there and then there, till we worked out an average speed from the hour of our departure that caused the skipper to swear if the 'Shark' was not already astern of us she could not be very far ahead, unless a great luck of wind had befallen her; a conjecture scarce fair to put down as a basis to build our figures upon, since it was a hundred to one that her fortune in the shape of breezes had been ours. For, be it remembered, we were in a well-scoured ocean; the winds even north of the 'rains' and 'horse-latitudes' were in a sense to be reckoned on, with the trades beyond as steady in their way as the indication of a jammed dogvane, and the 'doldrums' to follow—the equinoctial belt of catspaws and molten calms where one sailor's chance was another's the wide world round.

But so reasoned Finn, and I was not there to say him nay; yet it was difficult to hear him without a sort of mental shrug of the shoulders, though it was a talk to smooth down the raven plume of Wilfrid's melancholy 'till it smiled.' My cousin managed very well without his valet, protested indeed that he felt easier in his spirits since the fellow had gone forward, as though, all unconsciously to himself, he had long been depressed by the funeral face of the man.

'Besides,' said he, in his simple, knowing way, with a quivering of the lids that put an expression of almost idiot cunning into the short, pathetic peering of his large, protruding eyes, 'he was with me when my wife left my home; he it was who came to tell me that Lady Monson was not to be found; it was he, too, who put Hope-Kennedy's letter into my hand though it was picked up by one of the housemaids. These were thoughts that would float like a cloud of hellish smoke in my brain when he was hanging about me, and so I'm glad to have him out of my sight; yes,

I'm the better for his absence. And then,' he added, lowering his voice, 'his behaviour proves that he is not sound in his mind.'

That Muffin was as well content with the arrangement as his master I cannot say. They kept him at work forward upon small mean jobs, and he seldom came aft unless it was to lend a hand in pulling upon a rope. Yet after a little I would see him in a dog-watch on the forecastle with a huddle of seamen on the broad grin round him. One special evening I remember when the watch had run out into the dusk, and it might have been within half-an-hour of eight-bells, I arrived on deck from the dinner table and heard, as I supposed, a woman singing forward. The voice was a very good clear soprano, with a quality in it that might have made you imagine a middle-aged lady was tuning up. The song was 'The Vale of Avoca.' The concertina accompaniment was fairly played. I listened with astonishment, for some time wondering whether Miss Jennings' maid had got among the men, and then called to Crimp—

'Who's that singing?' said I.

'Him they've nicknamed the mute,' said he.

'What, Muffin?'

'Ay! sounds as if he'd swallowed his sister and she was calling out to be released.'

There happened inside this particular week with which I am dealing an incident much too curious not to deserve a place here. All day long it had been blowing a fresh breeze from north-east, but as the sun sank the wind went with him and about an hour before sunset there was a mild air breathing with scarce weight enough in it to blow the scent off a milkmaid, as sailors say, though it was giving the yacht way as you saw by the creep of the wrinkles at her stem working out from the shadow of the yacht's form in the water into lines that resembled burnished copper wire in the red western light. Miss Laura and Wilfrid were on deck, and I was leaning over the rail with a pipe in my mouth, all sorts of easy, dreamy fancies slipping into me out of the drowsy passage of the water alongside with its wreath of foam bells eddying or some little cloudy seething of white striking from our wet and flashing side into a surface which hung so glass-like with the crimson tinge in the atmosphere sifting down into it that you fancied you could see a hundred fathoms deep. Presently running my eyes ahead I caught sight of some minute object three or four points away on the weather bow, which every now and again would sparkle like the leap of a flame from the barrel of a musket. I stepped to the companion, picked up the telescope and made the thing out to be a bottle, the glass of which gave back the sunlight in fitful winkings to the twists and turns of it upon the ripples.

'What are you looking at?' cried Wilfrid.

'A bottle,' I answered.

'Ho!' he laughed, 'what you sailors call a dead marine, ha? What sort of liquor will it have contained, I wonder, and how long has it been overboard?'

The glass I held was Captain Finn's; it was a very powerful instrument, and the bottle came so close to me in the lenses that it was like examining it at arm's length.

'It is corked,' said I.

'Can we not pick it up?' exclaimed Miss Jennings.

'Oh, but an empty bottle, my dear,' exclaimed Wilfrid, with a shrug.

I examined it again. 'I tell you what, Wilfrid; that it is corked should signify there is something in it. Who troubles himself to plug an empty bottle when it is flung overboard unless it is intended as a messenger?'

He was instantly excited. 'Why, by all means then——,' he broke off, looking round. The mate had charge; he was sulkily pacing the deck to leeward with a lift of his askew eye aloft and then a stare over the rail, all as regular as the recurrence of rhymes in poetry. 'Mr. Crimp,' called Wilfrid. The man came over to us. 'Do you see that bottle?'

Crimp shaded his eyes and took a steady view of the water towards which my cousin pointed, and then said, 'Is that there thing flashing a bottle?'

'Yes, man; yes.'

'Well, I see it right enough.'

'Get it picked up, Mr. Crimp,' said Wilfrid.

The mate walked aft. 'Down hellum,' he exclaimed to the fellow who was steering. The wheel was put over and the bottle was brought almost directly in a line with the yacht. The topgallantsail 'lifted,' but what air blew was abaft the beam and the distance was too short to render necessary the handling of the braces and sheets. Crimp went a little way forward and hailed the forecastle, and presently a man stood ready at the gangway with a canvas bucket slung at the end of a line. A very small matter will create a great deal of interest at sea Had the approaching bottle been a mermaid the group of sailors could not have observed it with livelier attention nor awaited its arrival with brisker expectations. Presently *splash*! the bottle was cleverly caught, hauled up, dried and brought aft.

'It's not been in the water long,' said I; 'the wooden plug in the mouth looks fresh.'

'Mr. Crimp, sing out for a corkscrew,' cried Wilfrid.

'No good in that,' cried I; 'break the thing. That will be the speediest way to come at its contents.'

I held the bottle to the sun a moment, but the glass was thick and black, and revealed nothing. I then knocked it against the rail, the neck fell and exposed a letter folded as you double a piece of paper to light your pipe with. I pulled it out and opened it; Miss Laura peeped over one shoulder, Wilfrid over the other; *his* respirations swift, almost fierce. It was just the thing to put some wild notions about the 'Shark' into his head. From the forecastle the sailors were staring with all their eyes. The paper was quite dry; I opened it carefully with an emotion of awe, for trifling as the incident was apparently, yet to my fancy there was the mystery and the solemnity of the ocean in it too. Indeed, you thought of it as having something of the wonder of a voice speaking from the blue air when your eye sought the liquid expanse out of whose vast heart the tiny missive had been drawn. It was a rude, hurried scrawl in lead pencil, and ran thus:

'*Brig Colossus George Meadows, Captain.*

*Vaterlogged five days—all hands but two dead; 'ast breaking up. No fresh water. Raw pork ne cask. Who finds this for God's sake report.'*

The word September was added, but the writer iad omitted the date, probably could not emember it after spelling the name of the nonth. I gave Crimp the note that he might ake it forward and read it to the men, telling iim to let me have it again.

'They will all have perished by this time, no loubt,' said Wilfrid in his most raven-like note.

'Think of them with raw pork only! The neat crystallised with salt, the hot sun over heir heads, not a thimbleful of fresh water, the essel going to pieces plank by plank, the horrible nguish of thirst made maddening by the mockery of the cold fountain-like sounds of that brine there lowing in the hold or washing alongside with a hampagne-like seething! Oh,' groaned I, 'who s that home-keeping bard who speaks of the ocean as the mother of all? The mother! A tigress. Why, if old Davy Jones be the devil, Jack is right in finding an abode for him down on the ooze there. Mark how the affectionate mother of all torments its victims with a hellish refinement of cruelty before strangling them! how—if the land be near enough—she will fling them ashore, mutilated, eyeless, eaten, in horrid triumph and enjoyment of her work, that we shuddering radishes may behold and understand her power.'

'Cease, for God's sake!' roared Wilfrid; 'you're talking a nightmare, man! Isn't the plain fact enough?' he cried, picking up the broken bottle and flinging it in a kind of rage overboard, 'why garnish?'

'I want to see the ocean properly interpreted,' I cried. 'Your poetical personifications are claptrap. Great mother, indeed! Great grandmother, Wilfrid. Mother of whales and sharks, but when it comes to man——'

'Oh, but this is impiety, Mr. Monson,' cried Miss Laura, 'it is really dangerous to talk so. One may *think*—but here we are upon the sea, you know, and that person you spoke of just now (pointing down) might with his great ears——'

'Now, Laura, my dear,' broke in Wilfrid, 'can't we pick up a wretched bottle and read the melancholy message it contains without falling ill of fancy?' He went to the skylight—'Steward, some seltzer and brandy here! Your talk of that salt pork,' he continued, coming back to us, 'makes my tongue cleave to the roof of my mouth. I would give much for a little ice, d'ye know. Heigho! Big as this ocean is, I vow by the saints there's not room enough in it for the misery there is in the world!' with which he set off pacing the deck, though he calmed down presently over a foaming glass; but he showed so great a dislike to any reference to the bottle and its missive that, to humour him, Miss Jennings and I forbore all allusion to the incident.

It was next forenoon, somewhere about the hour of eleven o'clock, that the lookout man on the topgallantyard—whom I had noticed playing for some time the polished tubes, which glanced like fire in his lifted hands as he steadied the glass against the mast—suddenly bawled down with a voice of excitement, 'Sail ho!'

Wilfrid, who was lounging on the skylight, jumped off it; I pricked up my ears; Miss Laura hollowed her gloved hands to take a view of the man aloft.

'Where away?' cried Finn.

'Right ahead, sir.'

'What do you make her out to be?'

The seaman levelled the telescope again, then swinging off from the yard by his grip of the tie, he sung out, 'She looks to be a wreck, sir. I don't make out any canvas set.'

'She'll be showing afore long, your honour,' said Finn, and he cast his eye upon the water to judge of our speed.

All night long it had blown a weak wind, and the draught was still a mere fanning, with a hot sun, that made the shelter of the awning a necessary condition of life on deck by day; a clear, soft, dark blue sky westwards, and in the east a broad shadowing of steam-like cloud with a hint in the yellow tinge of it low down upon the sea of the copper sands of Africa, roasting noons and shivering midnights, fever and cockroaches, and stifling cabins. So that, merely wrinkling through it as we were, it was not until we had eaten our lunch, bringing the hour to about a quarter before two o'clock, that the vessel sighted from aloft in the morning had risen above the rim of the ocean within reach of a glass directed at her over the quarterdeck rail.

'It will be strange,' said I, putting down the telescope after a long stare at her, 'if yonder craft don't prove the "Colossus." Look at her, Wilfrid. A completer wreck never was.'

He seized the glass. 'By George, then,' he cried, 'if that's so the two men that paper spoke of may be still alive. I hope so, I hope so. We owe heaven a life, and it is a glorious thing to succour the perishing.' His hand shook with excitement as he directed the glass at the vessel.

Points of her stole out as we approached. She had apparently been a brig. Both masts were gone flush with the deck, bowsprit too, channels torn from their strong fastenings, and whole lengths of bulwark smashed level. I supposed her cargo to have been timber, but her decks showed bare, whence I gathered that she was floating on some other sort of light cargo—oil, cork; no telling what indeed. She swayed wearily upon the long ocean heave with a sulky, sickly dip from side to side, as though she rocked herself in her pain. There was a yard, or spar, in the water alongside of her, the rigging of which had hitched itself in some way about the rail, so that to every lurch on one side the boom rose half its length, with a flash of the sun off the wet end of it, and this went on regularly, till after watching it a bit I turned my eyes away with a shudder, feeling in a sense of creeping that possessed me for an instant the sort of craziness that would come into a dying brain aboard the craft to the horrible maddening monotony of the rise and fall of that spar.

'Such a picture as that,' whispered Miss Jennings softly in my ear, 'realises your idea of the ocean as a tigress. What but claws could have torn her so? And that soft caressing of the water—is it not the velvet paw stroking the dead prey?'

'There's a man on board!' cried Wilfrid wildly; 'look, Charles.'

He thrust the glass into my hand whilst he pointed with a vehement gesture. I had missed him before, but the broadside opening of the wreck to our approach disclosed his figure as he sat with folded arms and his chin on his breast in a sleeping posture against the companion that remained intact, though the wheel, skylight, and all other deck fixtures that one could think of were gone. I eyed him steadily through the lenses, but though he never raised his head nor stirred his arms, which lay folded, yet owing to the roll of the hulk it was impossible to say that his body did not move.

'There's the word "Colossus,"' said I, 'painted plainly enough upon her bow. Yonder may be the writer of the letter received. Wilf, you should send a boat. He may be alive—God knows! But though *he* be dead there might be another living.'

'Finn,' cried Wilfrid, 'bring the yacht to a stand and board that wreck instantly, d'ye hear?'

'Ay, ay, sir.'

'I'll make one of the boat's crew with your good leave, captain,' I sung out.

'Take charge by all means, Charles,' said Wilfrid.

'With pleasure,' said I. 'See two things in the boat, Finn, before we start—fresh water and a drop of brandy or rum.'

The yacht's topsail was backed, the helm put down and the vessel's way arrested. We came to a halt within half-a-mile of the wreck. The ocean swung smoothly in wide-browed folds that went brimming to the hulk in rounds polished enough at times to catch the image of her till she showed as she leaned from us with her reflection leaning too as if she had broken in halves and was foundering. The boat was lowered and brought to the gangway; I jumped in and we shoved off. Five fellows pulled, and on a sudden I had to turn my head away to smother a laugh whilst I seemed to wave a farewell to Wilfrid and Miss Laura on noting that one of the rowers was no less a man than Muffin. Whether he had thrust himself into this errand owing to some thirst for any momentary change in the discipline of his shipboard life, or whether Finn had remembered that the fellow talked much of being able to feather an oar and had ordered him into the boat, I cannot tell, but there he was, as solemn as a sleeping ape, his old straw hat pulled down to his nose and his eyes steadfastly fixed upon the oar that he plied. He pulled well enough, but his anxiety to keep time and to feather besides was exceedingly absurd, and it cost me no small effort to master my face, though the struggle to look grave and ignorant of his presence was mightily helped in a minute by the sight of the silent figure seated upon the wreck's deck.

I earnestly overhauled with my eyes the wallowing fabric as we approached her, but saving that lonely man motionless in his posture of slumber there was nothing to be distinguished outside the melancholy raffle of unrove rigging and ropes' ends in the bow, vast rents in the planks of the deck, splinters of bulwark, stanchion, and the like. The fellow that pulled stroke was the big-whiskered man that acted as boatswain, named Cutbill. I said to him as he came stooping towards me for the sweep of his oar, 'She's so jagged the whole length of her broadside, that I believe her stern, low as it lies, will be the easiest and safest road to enter by.'

He looked over his shoulder and said, 'Ay, sir. But there is no need for you to trouble to step aboard. I'll overhaul her if you like, sir.'

'No, I'll enter her. It's a break, Mr. Cutbill. But you will accompany me, for I may want help.'

He shook his head. 'You'll find nothing living there, sir.'

'No telling till we've found out anyway,' said I. 'Oars!' I sung out.

We floated under the wreck's counter, hooked on, and, waiting for the lift of the swell, I very easily sprang from the boat's gunwale to the taffrail of the hulk, followed by Cutbill. The decks had blown up, and the sort of drowning rolling of the hulk rendered walking exceedingly dangerous. The water showed black through the splintered chasms, with a dusky gleam in the swaying of it like window-glass on a dark night; and there was a strange noise of sobbing that was desperately startling, with its commingling of sounds like human groans, and hollow frog-like croakings, followed by blows against the interior caused by floating cargo driven against the side, as if the hull was full of half-strangled giants struggling to pound their way out of her.

From the first great gap I looked down through I remember recoiling with a wildness that might easily have rolled me overboard to the sight of a bloated human face, with long hair streaming, floating on the surface of the water athwart the ragged crifice. It was like putting one's eye to a *camera obscura* and witnessing a sickening phantom of death, saving that here the horror was real, with the weeping noises in the hold to help it, and the great encompassing sea to sweep it into one's very soul as a memory to ride one's sleepless hours hag-like for a long term.

We approached the figure of the man. He was seated on a three-legged stool, with his back resting against the companion. I stooped to look at his face.

'Famine is the artist here!' I cried instantly, springing erect. 'My God! what incomparable anguish is there in that expression!'

'See, sir,' cried the burly sailor by my side in a broken voice, and he pointed to a piece of leather that lay close beside the body. One end of it had been gnawed into pulp, which had hardened into iron again to the air and the sun.

'Yet the letter we picked up,' said I, 'stated there was a cask of raw meat on board.'

'*That* was chewed for thirst sir,—for thirst, sir!' exclaimed the seaman. 'I suffered once, and bit upon a lump of lead to keep the saliva a running.

'Best not linger,' said I. 'Take a look forward, will you?'

He went towards the forecastle; I peered down the little companion way; it was as black as the inside of a well, with the water washing up the steps within reach of my arm. There could be nothing living down there, nor indeed in any other part of the wreck if not on deck, for she was full of water. The men in the boat astern were standing up in her with their heads bobbing together over the line of the taffrail to get a view of the figure, for it was seated on the starboard side, plain in their sight, all being clear to the companion; yet spite of that lump of whiskered mahogany faces, with Muffin's yellow chops in the heart of it to make the whole group as commonplace as a sentence of his, never in all my time did so profound a sense of desolation and loneliness possess me as I stood bringing my eyes from the huge steeping plain of the sea to that human shape with its folded arms and its bowed head. Heavens, thought I, what scenes of human anguish have the ocean stars looked down upon! The flash past of the ghastly face in the hold beneath—that bit of gnawed leather, which even had you thought of a dog coming to such a thing would have made your heart sick—the famine in that bowed face where yet lay so fierce a twist of torment that the grin of it made the slumberous attitude a horrible sarcasm——

'Nothing to be seen, sir,' exclaimed Cutbill, picking his way aft with the merchantman's clumsy rolling step.

I went in a hurry to the taffrail and dropped into the boat, he followed, and the fellow in the bow shoved off. Scarce, however, had the men dropped their oars into the rowlocks, each fellow drawing in his breath for the first stretch back, when a voice hailed us from the deck:

'*For God's sake don't leave me!*'

'Oh!' shrieked Muffin, springing to his feet

and letting his oar slide overboard; 'there's someone alive on board!'

'Sit, you lubber!' thundered the fellow behind him, fetching him a chip on the shoulder that brought him in a crash to his hams, whilst the man abaft picked up the oar.

Every face wore an expression of consternation. Cutbill's, that looked like a walnut shell between his whiskers, turned of an ashen hue; he had stretched forth his arms to give the oar its first swing, and now they forked out paralysed into the stiffness of marline-spikes by astonishment.

'Smite my eyes,' he muttered as though whispering to himself, 'if it ain't the first dead man's voice *I* ever heard.'

'Back water!' I cried out, for the swell had sheered the boat so as to put the companion way betwixt us and the figure. I stood up and looked. The man was seated as before, though spite of the sure and dreadful expression of death his famine-white face bore, spite of my being certain in my own mind that he was as dead as the creature whose face had glimmered out upon the black water in the hold, yet the cry to us had been so unmistakably real, had come so unequivocally, not indeed only from the wreck, but from the very part of the hulk on which the corpse was seated, that I found myself staring at him as though I expected that he would look round at us.

'There's no one alive yonder, men,' said I, seating myself afresh.

'What was it that spoke, think 'ee, sir?' exclaimed the man in the bow, bringing his eyes full of awe away from the sheer hulk to my face.

'Mr. Monson, sir, I 'umbly beg pardon,' exclaimed Muffin, in the greasy deferential tone he was used to employ when in the cabin, 'but there must be something living on board that ship, unless it were a sperrit.'

'A spirit, you fool!' cried I in a passion, 'what d'ye mean by such talk? There's nothing living on that wreck, I tell you. Jump aboard anyone of you who doubts me and he can judge for himself.'

Muffin shook his head; the others writhed uneasily on the thwarts of the boat.

'Cutbill and I overhauled the vessel; she's full of water. What is on her deck you can see for yourselves, and nothing but a fish could live below. Isn't that right, Cutbill?'

'Ay, sir,' he answered; and then under his breath, 'but what voice was it that hailed us then?'

'Come, give way!' I cried, 'they'll be growing impatient aboard the yacht.'

The oars dipped, feathered, flashed, and in an instant the blue sides of the smart and sparkling little craft were buzzing and spinning through it in foam. It was like coming from a graveyard to the sight of some glittering, cheerful, tender poetic pageant to carry the eye from the hull to the yacht. She seemed clad by the contrast with new qualities of beauty. You found the completest expression of girlish archness in the curtseying of her shapely bows, with a light at her forefoot like a smile on the lip when she lifted her yellow sheathing there, pouting, as one might say, from the caressing kiss of the blue brine, to gleam like gold for a moment to the sunlight. We swept alongside and I sprang on board.

'The poor creature is dead, I suppose?' exclaimed Wilfrid, inspecting the wreck through a binocular glass.

'Yes,' I answered, 'dead as the dead can be; too dead to handle, faith. I might have sought in his pockets for some hints to found a report upon, but his face had the menace of a fierce whisper.'

'It seems cruel to leave him unburied,' said Miss Laura, with her soft eyes full of pity, and the emotions begotten of the presence of death.

'That hulk must soon go to pieces,' said I, 'and then she will give him a sailor's funeral.'

'When nature acts the part of high priestess,

if there be such a part,' exclaimed Wilfrid, in a low, tremulous voice, not without a kind of sweetness in its way, thanks, perhaps, to the mood of tender sentiment that was upon him, 'how grandly she celebrates the humblest sailor's obsequies! how noble is her cathedral! Observe the altitude of that stupendous roof of blue. How sublime are the symphonies of the wind; how magnificent the organ notes which they send pealing through this great echoing fabric! Nature will give yonder poor fellow a nobler funeral than it is in our power to honour him with. But Charles,' he cried, with a sudden change of voice, and indeed with a new manner in him, 'have you ever remarked the exquisite felicity with which nature invents and fits and works her puppet shows? Take yonder scene at which we have been suffered to steal a peep. What could be more choicely imagined than that a dead man should have charge of such a dead ship as that, and that the look-out he is keeping upon her deck should be as black as the future of the vessel he still seems to command?'

'Well, well,' said I, 'all this may be as you put it, Wilf. But all the same, I am glad to see that topsail yard swung and that spectre there veering astern. I protest my visit has made me feel as though I must lie down for a bit;' and, in sober truth, the body I had inspected, coupled with the thrill of amazement that had shot through me to the voice we had heard, had proved a trifle too much for my nerves, topped, as it all was, with certain superstitious stirrings, the crawling, as it might be, upon the memory of that ghostly, insoluble hail, along with the workings of an imagination that was too active for happiness when anything approaching to a downright horror fell in its way. So I went below and lay upon a sofa, but had scarcely hoisted my legs when Wilfrid arrived, bawling to the steward for a bottle of champagne, and immediately after came Miss Jennings, who must needs fetch me a pillow, and then, as though she had a mind to make me feel ridiculous, saturate a pocket handkerchief with eau de Cologne, all which attentions I hardly knew whether to like or not till, having swallowed a bumper of champagne, I hopped off the couch with a laugh.

'A pretty sailor I am, eh, Wilfrid?' cried I; 'a likely sort of figure to take command of the Channel Fleet. Miss Jennings, your eau de Cologne has entirely cured me.'

'What's to be the next incident now—the "Shark"?' exclaimed Wilfrid. He thrust his hands deep into his trousers pocket and marched into his cabin, head hanging down.

## CHAPTER XVI.

### WE SIGHT A SCHOONER-YACHT.

I HAPPENED to be alone on deck after dinner, having left Wilfrid at his diary and Miss Jennings in her cabin, where she had gone to make ready to join me, as she had said. The wreck had faded out before sundown, melting upon the flashing purple under the sinking luminary like the memory of a nightmare off a mind upon which is streaming a light of cheerfulness. The night was clear but dark, with a pleasant wind through whose dryness the stars looked down purely. The yacht was sailing a fair six knots, as I gathered when I stepped from the companion to the lee-rail and peered over in a wool-gathering way at the emerald gushings and eddyings of the phosphoric fires which winked in the cloudy paleness along the bends, and fled into the dimness of glow-worms to the spectral racing of our wake.

I was worried and oppressed by a sort of heaviness of spirits. I had acted a cheerful part at dinner, but there was little of my heart in the tongue I wagged. The recollection of the motionless figure seated upon the wreck, and darker yet, the memory of that bloated, long-haired phantom face sliding in the space of a breath across the gape in the shattered deck, with the sobbing wash of the black water on which it floated to put a dreadful meaning of its own into the livid, nimble vision went for something—nay, went for a good deal, no doubt; but it was the hail that had come from the wreck which mainly occasioned my perplexity and agitation, and, I may add, my depression. Twice now had syllables sounding from where there were no lips to pronounce them reached my ears. Had I alone heard them I should have been alarmed for my reason, not doubting an hallucination, though never for an instant believing in the reality of the utterance; but the voices had been audible to others, they were consequently real, and for that reason oppressive to reflect upon. The shadow of Wilfrid's craziness lay on his ship; the voyage was begun in darkness, and was an aimless excursion, as I thought, with no more reasonable motive for it than such as was to be found in the contending passions of a bleeding heart. Hence it was inevitable that any gloomy incident which occurred during such an adventure as this should gather in the eye of the imagination a very much darker tincture than the complexion it would carry under sunnier and more commonplace conditions of an ocean run.

Whilst I lay over the rail lost in thought, I was accosted by Finn.

'Beg pardon, Mr. Monson; couldn't make sure in this here gloom whether it was you or Sir Wilfrid. May I speak a word with 'ee, sir?'

'Certainly, Finn.'

'Well now, sir, if that there old Jacob Crimp ain't gone and took on so joyful a frame of mind that I'm a land-crab if his sperrits ain't downright alarming in a man whose weins runs lime-juice!'

'Old Crimp!' cried I, 'what's the matter with him?'

'Why, he comes up to me and says, "Capt'n," he says, "there's Joe Cutbill, Jemmy Smithers, that funeral chap Muffin, and the t'others who was in the boat which went to the wreck this afternoon, all a-swearing that they heard a voice in the air!" and so saying, he bursts out a laughing like a parrot. "A woice!" says he. "So me and Mr. Monson aren't the only ones, d'ye see. Damme," says he, "if it don't do my heart good to think on't. There's the whole bloomin' boiling of us now," says he, "to laugh at capt'n; not

Jacob Crimp only," and here he bursts into another laugh.'

'What does the old chap want to convey?' said I.

'Why, sir, joyfulness as that he no longer stands alone as having heard a woice, for though to be sure you was with him that night, and some sound like to a cuss rose up off yon quarter, he feels like being alone in the hearing of it, for, ye see, a man in his position can't comfortably hitch on to a gent like you, and it was the harder for him, for that the man at the wheel swore that he never heard the cry.'

'He is superstitious, like most old lobscousers, no doubt,' said I. 'Have the others been talking about this mysterious hail from the wreck?'

'Ay, sir; 'tis a pity. It's raised an oneasiness 'mongst the men. There's that Irish fool O'Connor, him that foundered the "Dago," going about with a face as long as a wet hammock and swearing that 'tain't lucky.'

'I don't know about its being unlucky,' said I, 'but it certainly is most confoundedly curious, Captain Finn.'

I saw him peering hard at me in the dusk. 'But surely your honour's not going to tell me there *was* a woice?' said he.

'As we were shoving off,' said I, 'we were hailed in God's name to return. Every man of us in the boat heard it. There were but two bodies in the wreck, as stone dead as if they had died before the days of the flood. What say you to *that*, Captain Finn?'

He pulled off his hat to scratch his head. After a pause, he exclaimed slowly, 'Well, I'm for leaving alone what isn't to be onderstood. There was ghosts maybe afore I was born, but none since; and the dead h'ant talked, to my knowledge, since New Testament times. Old Jamaicy rum isn't to be had by dropping a bucket over the side, and if a truth lies too deep to be fished up by creeps, better drop it, says I, and fix the attention on something else.'

'You tell me the men are uneasy?'

'Ay, sir.'

'Do you mean all hands?'

'Well, your honour knows what sailors are. When they're housed together under one deck they're like a box of them patent lucifer lights—if one catches, the whole mass is aflame.'

'It's a passing fit of superstition,' said I. 'Give it time. Best say nothing about it to Sir Wilfrid.'

'Bless us, no, sir. Sorry it's raised so much satisfaction in that there old Jacob, though. A laugh in Jacob don't sound natural. Any sort o' joyfulness in such a constitution is agin nature.'

At this point Miss Jennings arrived on deck, and Finn, with a shadowy fist mowing at his brow, stepped to the opposite rail, where his figure was easily distinguished by the stars he blotted out.

'I hope your spirits are better,' said Miss Laura.

'I should be glad to turn the silent sailor of that wreck out of my memory; but my spirits are very well.'

'Wilfrid noticed your depression at table, but he attributed it entirely to the dreadful sight you witnessed on the wreck.' She passed her hand through my arm with a soft impulse that started me into a walk, but there was so much real unconsciousness in her way of doing this—a child-like intimation of her wish to walk without proposing it, and so breaking the flow of our speech at the moment—that for some little while I was scarce sensible I held her arm, and that I was pacing with her. 'But I think there is more the matter with you, Mr. Monson,' she continued, with her face glimmering like pearl in the dusk, as she looked up at me, 'than meets the ear—I will not say the eye.'

'The fact is, Miss Jennings,' said I abruptly, 'I am bothered.'

'By what?'

'Well, what think you of the suspicion which grows in me that this yacht carries along with her, in the atmosphere that enfolds her, some sort of Ariel, whose mission it is to bewilder out of its invisibility the sober senses of men of plain, practical judgment, like your humble servant?'

'You want to frighten me by pretending that you are falling a little crazy.'

'No!'

'Or you are creating an excuse to return home.'

'No, again. How can I return home?'

'Why, by the first convenient ship we happen to sight and speak. Is this some stratagem to prepare Wilfrid's mind for your bidding us farewell when the chance happens?'

She spoke with a subdued note and a tremble of fretfulness in it.

'Suffer me to justify myself,' said I, and with that I led her to the captain, who stood with folded arms leaning against the rail near the main rigging. 'Finn!' He dropped his hands and stood bolt upright. 'Be so good as to tell Miss Jennings what the men are talking about forward.'

'You mean the woice, sir?'

'What the men are talking about,' said I.

'Well, miss,' said Finn, 'as the boat that Mr. Monson had charge of this afternoon was a-leaving the wreck the men heard themselves hailed by a woice that begged 'em, in God's name, not to leave the party as called behind. Mr. Monson, sir, you heard it likewise.'

'I did,' I answered.

'Another mystery,' exclaimed Miss Laura, 'quite as dismal and astonishing as Muffin's phosphoric warning.'

'Thanks, Finn; that's all I wanted to ask you,' said I, and we left him to resume our walk.

'Tell me about this voice,' said the girl.

I did so, putting plenty of colour into the picture, too, for I wanted her to sympathise with my superstitious mood, whilst up to now there was nothing but incredulity and a kind of coquettish pique in her voice and manner.

'And you are afraid of this voice, Mr. Monson? I wonder at you!'

'You should have my full consent to wonder,' said I, 'if it were the first time; but there was the other night, you know, with solid, sour, uncompromising old Crimp to bear me witness, and now again to-day, with a boatful of men for evidence.'

'Really, Mr. Monson, what do you want to make yourself believe?' she asked, with a tone like a half laugh in her speech; 'the dead cannot speak.'

'So 'tis said,' I grumbled, sucking hard at my cigar to kindle it afresh.

'Human syllables cannot be delivered save by human lips. What, then, could have spoken out of the darkness of the sea the other night?'

'Does not Milton tell of airy tongues that syllable men's names?' said I gloomily.

'Mr. Monson, I repeat that I wonder at you. How can you suffer your imagination to be cheated by some trick of the senses?' she laughed. 'Pray, be careful. You may influence me. Then what a morbid company shall we make? I am sure you would like me to believe in this mysterious voice of yours. But, happily, we Colonials are too young, as a people, to be superstitious. We must wait for our ruined castles, and our moated granges, and our long, echoing, tapestry-lined corridors. Then, like you English, we may tremble when we hear a mysterious voice.'

She started violently as she said this, giving my arm so smart a pull that it instantly brought me to a halt, whilst in a voice of genuine alarm she exclaimed, 'Good gracious! what is that?'

Her face was turned up towards the weather yardarm of the square topsail, where, apparently floating a little above the studdingsail-boom iron, like to a flame in the act of running down the smoke of an extinguished candle ere firing the wick, shone a pendulous bubble of greenish fire, but of a luminosity sufficiently powerful to distinctly reveal the extremity of the black spar pointing finger-like into the darkness ahead, whilst a large space of the curve of the topgallantsail above showed in the lustre with something of the glassy, delicate greenness you observe in a midsummer leaf in moonshine. The darkness, with its burden of stars, seemed to press to the yacht the deeper for that mystic light, and much that had been distinguishable outlines before melted out upon the sight.

'What is it?' exclaimed Miss Jennings in a voice of consternation, and I felt her hand tighten upon my arm with her fears thrilling through the involuntary pressure.

'Figure an echoing corridor hung with aged tapestry stirring to cold draughts which seem to come like blasts from a graveyard, a noise as of the distant clanking of chains, and then the apparition of a man in armour, holding up such a lantern as that yonder, approaching you who are spellbound and cannot move for horror.' I burst out laughing.

'What is that light, Mr. Monson?' she cried petulantly.

'Why,' Miss Jennings,' I answered, ''tis a saint, not a light; a reverend old chap called St. Elmo who transforms himself at pleasure into a species of snapdragon for the encouragement of poor Jack.'

'See that corposant, sir?' rumbled Finn out of the darkness.

'Very well, indeed,' I answered. 'Finn has explained,' I continued; 'that light is what sailors call a corpusant—sometimes compr*ee*sant. If we were Catholics of the Columbian period we should tumble down upon our knees and favour it with a litany or oblige it with a hymn; but being bleak-minded Protestants all that we can do is to wonder how the deuce it happens to be burning on such a night as this, for I have seen scores of these corposants in my time, but always either in dead calms or in gales of wind. But there it is, Miss Jennings, an atmospheric exhalation as commonplace as lightning, harmless as the glow-worm, though in its way one of the most poetic of old ocean's hundred suggestions; for how easy to imagine some giant figure holding that mystic lamp, whose irradiation blends the vast spirit shape with the gloom and blinds the sight to it, though by watching with a little loving coaxing of fancy one should be able after a bit to catch a glimpse of a pair of large sorrowful eyes or the outline of some wan giant face.'

'It is gone,' she exclaimed with a shudder.

'Hush!' I exclaimed, 'we may hear the rustling of pinions by listening.'

'Mr. Monson, you are ungenerous,' she cried with an hysterical laugh.

Suddenly the light glanced and then flamed at the foretopmast head, where it threw out, though very palely, the form of the lookout man on the topgallantyard, whose posture showed him to be crouching with his arm over his eyes.

'I dare say that poor devil up there,' I exclaimed, 'fully believes the fire-bubble to be a man's ghost.'

'It is a startling thing to see,' exclaimed Miss Jennings.

'But Colonials are too young as a people to be superstitious,' said I. 'It is only we of the old country, you know, with our moated granges——'

'What is the hour, Mr. Monson?'

'I say, Charles, are you on deck?' shouted Wilfrid from the companion hatch.

'Ay; here I am with Miss Jennings. What's the time, Wilfrid, d'ye know?'

As I spoke two silver chimes, and then a third, came floating and ringing from the forecastle—three bells, half-past nine.

'See that corposant?' bawled Wilfrid. And he came groping up to us. 'An omen, by George!' he cried with an odd hilarious note in his voice. 'Laura, mark me, that flame isn't shining for nothing. 'Tis a signal light fired by fortune to advise us of some great event at hand.'

'Quarterdeck there!' came down the voice of the lookout man, falling from sail to sail, as it seemed, in an echo that made the mysterious flame a wild thing to the imagination for a moment by its coming direct from it.

'Hallo?' roared Finn.

'Can I lay down till this here blasted light's burnt out? 'Tain't right to be all alone with it up here.'

'It *is* burnt out,' cried Finn, in a way which showed he sympathised with the fellow. In fact, as the sailor called the light vanished, and, though we stood looking awhile waiting for its reappearance, we saw no more of it.

That ocean corpse candle had shone at the right moment. Likely enough I should have made myself a bit merry over my tender and beautiful companion's fears in revenge for her pouting, pettish wonderment at the uneasiness which the mysterious voices had raised in me. But Wilfrid remained with us for the rest of the evening, and, as I was anxious that he should know nothing about the strange sound, I forbore all raillery. It was midnight when we went to bed. Our talk had been very sober, indeed somewhat philosophical in its way with its references to electrical phenomena. Wilfrid chatted with excitement, which he increased by two or three fuming glasses of seltzer and spirits. He told us a wild story of a ship that he was on board of somewhere down off the New Zealand coast, ploughing through an ocean of fire on a pitch-black night with a gale of wind blowing and a school of whales keeping pace with the rushing fabric, spouting vast feather-like fountains of burning water as they stormed through it. He talked like a man reciting a dream or delivering an imagination, and there was a passion in his speech due to excitement and old Cognac, along with a glow in his large peering eyes and a play of flushed features that persuaded me of a very defined mood of craziness passing over his mind. His fancy seemed to riot in the roaring, fiery scene he figured; the ship, plunging into hollows, which flashed about her bows like volcanic vomitings of flame, the heavens above black as soot, the ocean waving like sheet lightning to its confines, and the huge body of the whales crushing the towering surges as they rolled headlong through them into a moon-like brilliance, flinging on high their delicate emerald-green sparkling spouts of water, which floated comet-like over them against the midnight of the heavens.

On eight-bells striking we went to bed. All was quiet on deck; a pleasant breeze blowing under the hovering prisms and crystals of the firmament, the yacht leaning over in a pale shadow in the dusk and seething pleasantly along with a noise rising up from round about her like the rippling of a flag in a summer breeze. I fell asleep and slept soundly, and when I awoke it was to the beating of somebody's knuckles upon my cabin door. The day had broken, and my first glance going to the scuttle, I spied through the thick glass of it a windy sunrise with smoky crimson flakes and a tint of tarnished pink upon the atmosphere.

'Hallo! Hallo there! Who's that knocking?'

''Tis me, sir, Capt'n Finn. Can I have a word with your honour?' exclaimed the skipper, who had subdued his voice to a note that was alarming with its suggestion of physical effort.

'Come in, Finn. What is it now?'

The handle was turned, and the captain entered cap in hand. He closed the door carefully, and instantly said, 'Sorry to disturb you, sir, but baste me for an old duckling, Mr. Monson, if I don't believe the "Shark" to be in sight.'

'*What?*' I shouted, sitting bolt upright and flinging my legs over the edge of the bunk.

He glanced at the door, looking an intimation to me to make no noise. 'I thought I'd consult with 'ee first, sir, before reporting to Sir Wilfrid.'

'Is she in sight from the deck?'

'No, sir.'

'Have you seen her?'

'Ay, Mr. Monson, I'm just off the t'gallant-yard, where I've been inspecting her ever since she was first reported, and that'll be drawing on for five and twenty minutes.'

'But she is hull down?'

'Yes, sir, and still a schooner-yacht at that,' said he emphatically. 'Mind, I don't say she *is* the "Shark." All I want to report is a schooner with a yacht's canvas—not American cotton. No, sir, canvas like ourn, nothen square forrards, and sailing well she looks.'

'How heading?'

'Why to the south'ard and west'ard as we are. I'm in your hands, sir. It'll be a fearful excitement for Sir Wilfrid and a terrible blow if it's another vessel.'

'Oh, but you have to give him the news,

happen what will! Wait, however, till I have had a look, will you? I shall be with you in a minute or two.'

He left the berth, and in red-hot haste and with a heart beating with excitement I plunged into my clothes and ran on deck, passing softly, however, through the cabin; for, though I know not why it should be, yet I have observed that at sea there is something almost electrical in a time full of startling significance like this, an influence that, act as softly and be as hushed as you may, will yet arouse sleeping people and bring them about you in a dreaming way, wondering what on earth has happened. Pale and windy as the sunrise was, there was dazzle enough in the soaring luminary to stagger my sight on my first emergence. I stepped clear of the companion and stood whilst I fetched a few breaths gazing round me. The sea was a dull, freckled blue with a struggling swell underrunning it athwart the course of the wind as though the coming breeze was to be sought northwards. The horizon astern was gloomy and vague in the shadow of a long bank of clouds, a heap of sullen terraces of vapour rising from flint to saffron and then to a faint wet rose where the ragged sky line of the compacted body caught the eastern colour. All was clear water, turn where the gaze would. On the topgallantyard the fellow on the lookout lay over the spar with a telescope at his eye; his figure, as it swang through the misty radiance against the pale blue of the morning sky that south-east looked to be kindling into whiteness, was motionless with the intentness of his stare. If what the tubes were revealing to him was the "Shark," then, as he had been the first to sight her, that glittering heavy five-guinea piece nailed to the mainmast was his. It was as much the thought of this reward going from them as curiosity that had sent the watch on deck aloft too to have a look. The last of them was coming down hand over hand as I went forward. Discipline was forgotten in the excitement of such a moment as this, and swabs and squiligees had been flung down without a word of rebuke from Cutbill whose business it was to superintend the washing of the decks.

I sprang into the foreshrouds, and was presently alongside the lookout fellow. 'Give me hold of that glass,' said I. To the naked eye up here the sail hung transparently visible upon the edge of the sea, a point of lustrous white like the head of a marble obelisk lustrous with the silver of sunrise. But the telescope made a deal more of that dash of light than this. I threw a leg over the yard, steadied the glass against the mast, and instantly witnessed the white canvas of what seemed unquestionably a large schooner-yacht risen to her rail upon the horizon where the thin black length of her swam like an eel with the fluctuations of the refractive atmosphere; but all above was the steady brilliant whiteness of the cloths of the pleasure ship mounting from boom to gaff; a wide and handsome spread with a flight of triangular canvas hovering between jib-boom and topmast as though a flock of seafowl were winging past just there.

'Do you know the "Shark"?' said I to the man.

'I've seen her once or twice at Southampton, sir.'

'Is that she, think you?'

'Ay, sartin as that there water's salt.'

'Well, there'll be good pickings for you on the mainmast,' said I, handing him back the glass.

His face seemed to wither up between his whiskers to the incredible wrinkles of the smile which shrunk it to the aspect of an old dried apple. I got into the rigging and descended to the deck. The sailors stared hard at me as I went aft. I suppose they imagined that I was well acquainted with the 'Shark,' and they eyed my countenance with a solicitude that was almost humorous. Finn stood near the main rigging perspiring with impatience and anxiety, fanning his long face with his cap and sending glances in the direction of the sea, where presently those two alabaster-like spires now hidden would be visible.

'Is it the "Shark," think 'ee, sir?' he cried in a breathless way.

'My good Finn, how the dickens should I know? I know no more of the "Shark" than of Noah's Ark. But, seeing that the vessel we want is a schooner of some two hundred tons, of a fore and aft rig, bound our way, and a yacht to boot, then, if yonder little ship be not the chap we are in search of, this meeting with her will be an atrociously strange coincidence.'

'Just what I think, sir,' he cried, still breathless.

'Do you mean to shift your helm for her?'

'She was abeam when first sighted, sir. I have brought her on the bow since then, as ye can see. But I'll head straight if ye should think proper,' he exclaimed with a look aloft and around.

'Oh, by all means go slap for her, captain!' said I. 'That you know will be my cousin's first order.'

'Trim sail the watch!' he bawled out.

The helm was put over and the yacht's head fell off till you saw by the line of the flashing glass through which the fellow aloft continued to peer that the hidden sail had been brought about two points on the lee bow. All was now bustle on deck with trimming canvas, setting studdingsails, and the like. The dawn had found us close hauled with the topgallantsail lifting and every sheet flat aft, and now we were carrying the wind abaft the beam with a subdued stormy heave of the yacht over the sulky swell. Indeed, Finn should have made sail to the first shift of helm; but the poor fellow seemed to have lost his head till he had talked with me, scarce knowing how to settle his mind as to the right course to be instantly adopted in the face of that unexpected apparition which was showing like a snow-flake from aloft. For my part, I thought, I could not better employ the leisure that yet remained than by preparing for what was to come by a cold brine bath. So down I went, telling Finn that I would rout out Sir Wilfrid as I passed through the cabin and give him the news.

## CHAPTER XVII.

### WE RISE THE SCHOONER.

I DESCENDED into the cabin, walked straight to the door of Wilfrid's berth and knocked.

'Who's there?'

'I, Charles. I have news for you.'

'Come in, come in!'

I entered and found Wilfrid in his bunk propped up on his elbow, his eyes looking twice their natural size with the intensity of his stare, and one long uncouth leg already flung over the edge so that his posture was as if he had been suddenly paralysed whilst in the act of springing on to the deck.

'What news in the name of heaven? Quick, now, like a dear boy!'

'There's a schooner-yacht uncommonly like your "Shark" away down on the lee bow visible from aloft.'

He whipped his other leg out of bed and sat bolt upright. I had expected some extravagance of behaviour in him on his hearing this, but greatly to my surprise he sat silent in his bunk eyeing me, his brow dark and his lips moving for several seconds which might have been minutes for the time they seemed to run into.

'What is to-day, Charles?'

'Thursday.'

'Ha! It should be Monday. That light last night was an omen, as I told you. I knew some great event could not be far off.' His eyes kindled under their quivering lids and an odd smile twisted his mouth into the expression of a sarcastic grin. It was as ugly a look in him as I had ever seen, and it gained heavily in the effect it produced by his comparatively quiet manner.

'We are heading directly for her, of course?'

'Finn has her about two points on the lee bow,' said I.

'Will that do?' he exclaimed.

'Why, yes; hold a weather-gage of the chase, it is said; though I think we shall be having a northerly blast upon us before the sun touches his meridian.'

'Is she the "Shark," Charles?'

'You know I never saw the vessel, Wilf. But Finn and the chap on the yard seem to have no doubt of her, and the skipper ought to know anyway.'

On this he leapt to the deck with a *cry* of laughter, and coming up to me let fall his hand heavily upon my shoulder with such a grip of it that, spite of my having my coat on, it ached after he had let go like an attack of rheumatism. 'Now what say you?' said he, stooping, for he was a taller man than I, and peering and grinning close into my face. 'You looked upon this chase as a crazy undertaking, didn't you? The sea was such a mighty circle, Charles! the biggest ship in the world but an insignificant speck upon it, hey?'

He let go of me and brought his hands together, extending and slowly beating the air with them, with his body rocking. I awaited some passionate outfly, but whether his thoughts were too deep for words or that he was satisfied to think what at another time he might have stormed out with, he held his peace. Presently and very suddenly he abandoned his singular attitude and fell to collecting articles of his clothing which he pulled on as though he would tear them to pieces.

'I'll be with you on deck immediately,' said I, going to the door. But he did not seem to know that I was present; all the time he strained and dragged at his clothes he talked to himself rapidly, fiercely; pausing once to smite his thigh with his open hand; following this on with a low, deep laugh, like that of a sleeper dreaming.

Well, thought I as I stepped out and went to my berth, whether it prove the 'Shark' or not we shall have to 'stand by,' as Finn hinted, for some queer displays to-day. I met Miss Jennings' maid in the cabin and asked if she was going to her mistress. She replied yes. 'Then,' said I, 'give her my compliments and tell her that we have raised a large schooner-yacht during the night, and that Finn seems to think she is the "Shark."'

As I entered my berth I caught myself smiling over my fancy of the look that would come into the sweet girl's face when her maid gave her the message; the brilliant gleam of mingled alarm, temper, astonishment in her eyes, the sudden flush of her cheek and its paleness afterwards, the consternation in the set of her lips and the agitation of her little hands like the fluttering of falling snow-flakes as she dressed. But in good sooth I too was feeling mightily excited once more; I had cooled down somewhat since going on deck and viewing the distant sail from the masthead; now that I was alone and could muse, my pulse rose with my imaginations till it almost came to my thinking of myself as on the eve of some desperate and bloody business, boarding a pirate, say, with the chance of a live slow match in his magazine, or cutting out something heavily armed and full of men under a castle bristling with artillery. Supposing the craft to be the 'Shark,' what was to be the issue? The 'Bride' would be recognised; and Hope-Kennedy was not likely, as I might take it, to let us float alongside of him if he could help it. Suppose we maimed her and compelled her to bring to; what then? I had asked Finn this question long before, and he had said it would not come to a hand-to-hand struggle. But how could he tell? If we offered to board they might threaten to fire into us, and a single shot, let alone a wounded or a killed man, might raise blood enough to end in as grim an affray as ever British colours floated over. Small wonder that my excitement rose with all these fancies and speculations. And then again, supposing the stranger to be the 'Shark,' there was (to me) the astonishing coincidence of falling in with her—picking her up, indeed, as though we had been steered dead into her wake by some spirit hand instead of blundering on her through a stroke of luck, which had no more reference to Finn's calculations, and suppositions and hopings, than to the indications of the nose of our chaste and gilded figure-head.

When I went on deck I spied Wilfrid coming down the fore-rigging. He held on very tightly and felt about with his sprawling feet with uncommon cautiousness for the ratlines ere relaxing his grip of the shrouds. Finn was immediately under him, standing by, perhaps, to shoulder him up if he should turn dizzy. They reached the deck and came aft.

'She's not yet in sight from the cross-trees,' exclaimed Wilfrid, puffing and irritable from nervousness and exertion and disappointment, 'and I can't climb higher.'

'If she's the "Shark,"' said I, 'you're not going to raise her upon the horizon as if she were a beacon. But there's a spread of wings here that *she* can't show anyhow, and it will be strange if her white plumes are not nodding above that blue edge by noon.'

'Ay, sir,' rumbled Finn, 'specially with that coming along,' pointing to the North, where the weather looked heavy and smoky and thunderous with a purple rounding of shadow upon the sea-line and a hot-looking copperish light flowing off the jagged summits into the dusty blue as though it were sundown that was reflected there, whilst the troubled roll of the swell out of the shadow on the ocean put a finishing touch to the countenance of storm you found spreading astern from north-east to north-west. 'There'll be wind enough there, sir,' said Finn, keeping his square-ended stumpy fore-finger levelled, 'to give us white water to above our bow ports anon, or I'm a codfish.'

Wilfrid turned about and fell to pacing the deck; he struck out as though walking for a wager, tossing his legs and swinging his arms and measuring the planks from the wheel to very nearly abreast of the galley. Such of the sailors as were to windward slided to the other side, where you saw them exchanging looks though there was no want of respect in their manner, but on the contrary an air of active sympathy as if they were getting to master the full meaning of the existence of that sail below the horizon by observing how the report of it worked in the baronet.

'We must try and raise her,' muttered Finn in my ear, 'if only to pacify his honour by the sight of her. He can't climb, and he'll go out of himself if he don't see her soon.'

'But do you gain on her?'

'Why, yes, she is visible from the cross-trees already. But Sir Wilfrid can't get so high.' Well, thought I, this should surely signify slower heels than the 'Shark' is allowed to have.

I went to the taffrail and overhung it, watching the sky astern with an occasional mechanical glance at the wool-white spin of the wake gushing over the surface of the jumble of the swell like steam from the funnel of a locomotive. It was blowing a fresh wind, though I guessed it would slacken away soon to pipe up in a fresh slant presently. The yacht was a great fabric of cloths, every stitch abroad that would hold air, and she drove through it humming, troubled as she was by the irregular heave of the sea. In fact her movements were so awkward as to render walking inconvenient, and nothing, I believe, but the not knowing what he was about could have furnished Wilfrid with his steady shanks that morning. It was like a bit of sleep-walking, indeed, where a man who awake could not look down forty feet without desiring to cast himself out of a window, safely and exquisitely treads a narrow ledge of roof as high as the top of London Monument.

I was startled from my reverie by an exclamation, and turning, saw him hastily approaching Miss Jennings, who had just arrived on deck. He came to her with his arms extended as though he would embrace her.

'Laura, have you heard?'

'*Is* it the "Shark," Wilfrid?'

'Finn says yes. She exactly answers to the "Shark's" description. Hereabouts she should be, this is her track,—yes, yes, it is the "Shark." Would God it were Monday!' Then, seeing me looking, he bawled, 'Eh, Charles, what other ship should she prove? Fore and aft—fore and aft, of the "Shark's" burthen, as you and Finn say, a schooner, a pleasure craft by the colour of her canvas—' his face suddenly darkened, and he said something to Miss Jennings, but what I could not gather. She half turned away as if overcome by a sudden sense of sickness or faintness; the effect of some expression of fierce joy, I dare say, on his part, some savage whisper of assurance that his opportunity was not far distant now which acted upon her nervous system that trembled yet to the surprise of the news I had sent her through her maid. There was something so sad and appealing in her beauty just then that but for the feelings it possessed me with I might scarcely have suspected what a lover's heart I already carried in my breast for her. The troubled sweetness of her glances, her pale cheeks and lips, the swift rise and fall of her bosom, betokened consternation and the conflict of many emotions and, as I could not but think, a subduing sense of loneliness. Well, I must say I loved her the better for this weakness of spirit, for this recoil from the confrontment that she had been endeavouring to persuade herself she was looking forward to with a longing for it only a little less venomous than Wilfrid's. Nothing, I had thought again and again, but the soul of a fond, tender, chaste woman, gentle in mind and of a nature loveable, with the the best weaknesses of her sex, could go clad in such graces as she walked in withal from her topmost curl of gold to the full, firm, elegant little foot on which she seemed to float to the buoyant measures of the yacht's deck.

Wilfrid addressed her again hurriedly and eagerly with the gesticulations of a Jew in a passion. She answered softly, continuously sending scared looks over the yacht's bow. I heard him name his wife, but it was not for me to join them nor to listen, so I overhung the taffrail afresh, observing that even now there was a noticeable weakening in the weight of the wind, whilst the swing of the swell from a little to the westward of north was growing more regular, a longer and fuller heave with an opalescent glance in the vapour immediately over the sea-line as though the weather was clearing past the rim of the ocean.

'Mr. Monson.'

I turned. Miss Laura stood by my side. Wilfrid had left the deck. 'Is that vessel, that is said to be ahead of us, the "Shark," do you think?'

'I wish I knew positively for your sake, that I might relieve your anxiety.'

'If she should prove to be the vessel that my sister is in'—she drew a long, tremulous breath—'it will be a marvellous meeting, for I feel *now* as you have felt all through—now that that yacht is in sight from the mast up there—that this ocean is a vast wilderness.' She slowly ran her eyes, which were still charged with their scared look, along the sea-line.

'Well, Miss Jennings, hanging and marriage go by destiny, they say, and so does chasing a wife at sea apparently. I give you my word I am so excited I can scarcely talk.'

'But it may not be the "Shark."'

'Why, no.'

'I hope it is not,' she cried, starting to the rise in her voice with a glance at the helmsman, who stood near us.

'I can see that in your face,' said I.

'Oh, I hope it is not, and yet I want it to be the "Shark" too. Wilfrid must recover Henrietta. But it makes my heart stand still to think of our meeting. Oh, her shame! her shame! and then to find *me* here. And what is to happen?'

'Best let that craft turn out to be the "Shark" though,' said I. 'Here we are with a programme of rambles that threatens the world's end if we don't fall in with the Colonel. Keep your heart up,' said I gently. 'What have you to fear? It is for the galled jade to wince. Why t'other night you would have shot Hope-Kennedy had he stood up before you.'

She tried to smile, but the movement of her

lips swiftly faded out into their expression of grief and consternation.

'I will play my part,' she exclaimed, twisting her ring upon her finger. 'If my sister refuses to leave Colonel Hope-Kennedy I have made up my mind not to leave *her*. Where she goes I'll go.'

'I hope not,' I interrupted, 'for it might come, Miss Jennings, to my saying that where you go *I'll* go, and the Colonel may have rather curious views on the subject of guests.'

'You said you were too excited to talk,' she exclaimed with a little colour mounting. 'It may be that I am stupidly influenced by old memories. I was always afraid of Henrietta. She had an imperious manner, and an old lord whom I met at your cousin's—I forget his name—told Wilfrid that her eyes made him think of Mrs. Siddons in her finest scenes. I fear her influence upon me when I begin to entreat her. I know how she will look.'

'All this is mere nervousness,' said I. 'You thought of these things before, yet you are here. Besides, the sense of wrong-doing will mightily weaken the genius of wizardry in her—her power at least of exercising it and subduing by it—subduing even you, the tenderest and gentlest of girls; or depend on't she's no true member of your sex, but one of those demon-women whom Coleridge describes as wailing for their, or rather in her case for *new*, lovers.'

She made no reply. Shortly afterwards the breakfast bell summoned us below.

At table Wilfrid spoke little, but his manner was collected; whether it was that excitement was languishing in him or that he had managed to master himself, what he said was rational, his words and manner unclouded by that hectic which was wont to give the countenance of a high fever to all he said and did when anything happened to stir him up. He was stern and thoughtful, and it was easy to see that he accepted the vessel ahead as the 'Shark,' and that he was settling his plans. I was heartily grateful for this posture in him. I never knew anyone so fatiguing with his restlessness as my cousin. Half an hour of his company when he was much excited left one as tired, dry, and hollow as a four hours' argument with an illogical man. He was too much preoccupied to notice how pale and subdued and scared Miss Laura was, struggle as she might in his presence to seem otherwise. I talked very cautiously for fear of provoking a discussion that might heat him. Once he asked me in an angry, twitting way, as though to the heave-up within him of a sudden mood of wrath with a parcel of words atop which were bound to find the road out, whether I felt disposed *now* to challenge his judgment, whether I was still of opinion that the ocean was too wide a field for such a chase as this, and so on, proceeding steadily but with rising warmth through the catalogue of my early objections to the voyage; but instead of answering him I praised the bit of virgin corned beef off which I was breakfasting, wondered why it was that poultry was always insipid at sea, and so forced him back into his dark and collected silence or obliged him to quit his subject.

However, his inability to keep his attention long fixed helped me here, for he never attempted to pick up the end of the thread I had cut, though, little as he spoke, two-thirds of what he delivered himself of might have been worked into hot arguments but for my cautious answers.

I was not surprised on going on deck to find the wind no more than a light draught with the main boom swinging to the long roll of the yacht and the canvas flapping with vicious snaps at sheet and yard-arm. The water seemed to wash thick as oil from the yacht's sides, a dirty blue that went into an oozy sort of green northwards. There was a deadness in the lift of the swell that made you think of an idiot shouldering his way through a crowd, and the eye sought in vain for a streak of foam for the relief of the crisp vitality of it.

'Is that wind or thunder, think you, Mr. Crimp?' said I to the mate, whom I found in charge, whilst I pointed to the heaped-up folds of cloud astern, the brows of which were not far off the central sky that, spite of the sunshine, was blurred to the very luminary himself with the shadow in the north and with tatters and curls and streaks of rusty brassish vapour risen off the line of the main body and sulkily floating southwards.

'Wind or thunder?' answered Crimp with a dull, indifferent look; 'well, 'tain't tufted enough for thunder, but there'll be a breeze, I allow, behind this here swell.'

'Are we rising the chap ahead?'

'Not noticeably. She'll have to shift her hellum for us for that to happen at this pace,' sending an askew glance over the side. I was leaving him. 'Heard any more woices?' he asked.

'No, have you?'

'No, and don't want to. It's been a puzzling me, though,' he exclaimed, mumbling over a quid the juice of which had stained the corners of his mouth into so sour a sneer that no artist could have painted it better. 'Tell'ee what it is. I'm agoing to believe in ghosts.'

'You can't do better,' said I; 'get hold of a ghost and it will explain everything for you.'

'Well, 'tain't a childish notion anyhow. There's first class folks as believes in sperrits. What's a ghost like? Ne'er a man as I've asked forrads knows saving the mute, who describes it as a houtline.'

'What's inside his outline?' I asked.

'Why, that there Muffin can't get further than that. I says to him, how can a houtline speak? Look here, says he, answer me this: suppose ye takes a bottle and sucks out all the air from inside of it, what's left? A wacuum says I. And what's a wacuum? says he. Why, I says, says I, space, ain't it? I says. And what's space? says he. Why nothen, I suppose, I says, says I. Then says he, how can nothen exist? And yet, says he, it do exist, because ye can point to the bottle and say there it is. So with a ghost, says he; it's a houtline with nothen inside it if you like, but it's as real in its emptiness as the inside of a bottle with nothen in it.'

At any other time I should have hugely enjoyed an argument with this acrid old sailor on such a subject as ghosts. There is no company to my taste to equal that of a sour, prejudiced, ignorant salt of matured years, whose knowledge of life has been gained by looking at the world through a ship's hawse pipe, and who is full to the throat with the sayings and the superstitions of the forecastle. Jacob Crimp was such a man. Indeed he was the best example of the kind that I can recollect, thanks, perhaps, to the help he got from his queer sea-eyes, glutinous in appearance as a jellyfish, one peering athwart the other with a look of quarrelling about them that most happily corresponded with the sulky expression of his face and the growl of his voice that was like a sea blessing. But it was impossible to think of the schooner ahead and talk with this man about ghosts. I left him and got into the fore-shrouds and ascended to the cross-trees, where, receiving the glass from the fellow on the yard above, I took a view of the sea over the bow, and caught plainly the canvas of the vessel we were heading for,—her mainsail visible to the boom of it with a glimpse of her bowsprit end wriggling off into the dusky blue air at every rise of her bow to the lift of the swell. I noticed, however, that she had taken in her main gaff topsail, possibly with an eye to the weather astern; but it was a thing to set me problemising. Supposing her to be the 'Shark,' either she had not yet sighted us or she had no suspicion of us. Fidler, her captain, would, when we showed fair, be pretty sure to twig us by our rig; but was it likely that the Colonel and Lady Monson would gravely suppose that Wilfrid had started in chase of them? That, indeed, might depend upon whether her ladyship had missed the Colonel's letter to her, which my cousin had asked me to read. Well, we should have to wait a little. My heart beat briskly as I descended to the deck. Put yourself in my place, and think of the sort of excitement that was threatened before that morning sun shining up there had set!

Half an hour later the weak draught had died out; the rolling of the 'Bride' was putting a voice of thunder into her canvas, and the strain on hemp and spar presently obliged old Crimp to take in his studdingsails, which he followed on by ordering the topgallantsail to be rolled up and the gaff topsail hauled down. Wilfrid, who had arrived on deck, stood haggardly eyeing these manœuvres, but he said nothing, contenting himself with an occasional look, as dark as the shadow astern of us, at the weather there, and a fretful stride to the rail and a stormy stare at the sallow oil-smooth water that came swelling to the counter and washing the length of the little ship in a manner that made her stagger at times most abominably.

'Let that vessel prove what she may,' said I, sitting down on a grating abaft the wheel close to which he was standing, 'we appear to have the heels of her in light airs, however it may be with her in a breeze of wind.'

'How do you know?' he inquired in a churchyard note.

'Why,' said I, 'I was just now in the crosstrees and found her showing fair from them, whereas before breakfast she was only visible from the topgallantyard.'

He looked at me with a heavy, leaden eye, and said, 'A plague on the wind! It has all gone; just when we want it too.'

'We shall have a capful anon,' I exclaimed; 'no need to whistle for it. Mark how it brightens down upon the sea-line yonder as that shadow floats upwards. That means wind enough to whiten this tumbling oiliness for us.'

He directed his gaze in a mechanical way towards the quarter in which I was looking, but said nothing. Miss Jennings came out of the companion. I took her hand and brought her to the grating.

'A strange, oppressive calm,' she cried; 'how sickly the sunshine is! Nature looks to be in as dull a mood as we are.'

'Wilf,' said I, 'if that schooner is the "Shark," what will you do?'

'What would *you* do?' he answered sternly,

as though he imagined I quizzed him, when God knows I was in a more sober and anxious humour than I can express.

'Well,' said I very quietly and gravely, 'when I got my yacht within reach of her glasses, if I could manage it, I should signal that I wanted to speak her.'

'Quite right; that's what I shall do,' said he.

'But after?' I exclaimed.

'After what?' he cried.

'Why, confound it, Wilf, suppose she makes no response, holds on all, as we say at sea, and bowls along without taking the slightest notice of us.'

He approached me close, laid his great hand upon my shoulder and thrust his long arm forth straight as a handspike pointing to the forecastle gun. '*There's* my answer to that,' he cried in my ear in a voice as disagreeable as the sound of a saw with irritability; 'you wished me to strike it down into the hold, d'ye remember? you were for ridiculing it from the moment of your catching sight of it; yet without that messenger to deliver my mind what answer would there be to the question you have just now put? Oh my God,' he suddenly cried, smiting his forehead, 'I feel as if I shall go mad.'

He crossed to the other side of the deck and

paced it alone. Miss Jennings was too much dejected by all this, by the excitement of the time, by nervousness, grief, anxiety, to converse; nor, indeed, was my mood a very sociable one. I procured a chair for her, and presently found myself alone, as Wilfrid was, wishing from the very bottom of my heart that Colonel Hope-Kennedy was hanged, her ladyship in a lunatic asylum, and myself in my old West End haunts again, though somehow a misgiving as to the accuracy of this last desire visited me on a sudden with the glance I just then happened to cast at Miss Laura, who sat with her hands folded upon her lap, her head bowed in a posture of meditation that took an indescribable character of pathos from the expression on her sweet face.

It was now a little after ten o'clock. Crimp, who was pacing near me that Wilfrid might have the whole range of the weather quarterdeck to himself, suddenly rumbled out, 'Here comes the wind at last!' The stern of the yacht was still upon the north, where, at the very verge of the waters which sluggishly heaved like molten lead under the dark canopy of vapour that overhung them, the sea was roughening and whitening to the whipping of wind which looked at that distance to be coming along in a straight line, though as it approached us I witnessed a strange effect of long fibrine feelers sweeping out of the hoarse and rushing ridges of foam which were seething towards us—like darting livid tongues of creatures hidden in the yeast behind tipped with froth that made one think of the slender stem of a vessel ripping through the surface. In a few minutes the boiling popple was all about us, hissing to our counter with a shriek of wind which flashed with such spite into the great space of mainsail and the whole spread of square topsail that the yacht for a moment was bowed down to her ways, fair as it took her on her quarter. An instant she lay so, then came surging back to an almost level deck with her rigging alive as with the ringing of bells, took a sudden plunge forward, throwing from either bow a mass of creaming sea the summit of which went spinning like a snowstorm ahead of her, then gathering impulse in a long, floating, launching plunge as it were, she went sliding through it faster and faster yet till she had a wake like a millrace in chase of her.

It was a scene full of the life and spirit and reality of the ocean after the spell of sulky calm with its dingy northern heaving of water and its haze of weak, moist sunlight in the south and east. Finn to the first of the blast came on deck and fell abawling, the sailors sprang from rope to rope with lively heartiness, the slack running gear blew out in semi-circles, which with the curve of the canvas and the lean of the masts as the yacht swept forward with the brine boiling high along her, gave a wild, expectant, headlong look to the whole rushing fabric, something indeed to make one fancy that the spirit of her owner, the expression of whose face had her own strained, eager, rushing air, so to speak, had passed into and vitalised her—mere structure of timber as she was—into passionate human yearnings.

## CHAPTER XVIII.

### IS SHE THE 'SHARK'?

It was not to prove a gale, though it would have been hard to guess what lay behind that dirty jumble of white and livid terraces which had been stealthily creeping all the morning zenithwards. The clouds scattered to the rush of the wind, the sun with a brightened disk leapt from one flying vaporous edge to another, dazzling out the snows of the dissolving seas till the eye reeled from the glare of the brilliant foam and the sharp and lovely sparkle of the pure dark blue between. Indeed, before long the wind steadied down into a noble sailing breeze with a piebald sky of warm and cheerful weather steadily swinging into the south-east, as though the whole heaven revolved from one quarter to another like a panorama on a cylinder. Wilfrid looked his wishes, but said nothing. He hung apart in a fashion that was the same as telling me to keep off, nor had he anything to say to Miss Jennings. Finn easily interpreting his master's face, piled cloths on the yacht till it seemed as though another rag would blow the whole lofty white fabric of canvas, tapering spar, and rigging clean over the bows. We fled along in thunder, and to every curtsey of the vessel's head the water recoiled in a roar of spume as far as the jibboom end, to speed aft as fast, you would have thought, as the eye could follow it, the swell washing to the counter as if to help her.

We held on in this way for some time, when suddenly Wilfrid, who had come to a stand at the weather rail and was looking ahead, bawled with the note of a shriek in his voice, 'Look!' and out sprang his long arm pointing directly on a line with our bowsprit.

'Ay, there she is, sure enough!' cried I, as I caught sight, to a floating lift of the deck at that moment, of the pearlish gleam of canvas of a milky brilliance slanting past the soft whiteness of a head of sea against the marble look of the sky there, where the sun-touched clouds were going down to the ocean edge in a crowd with a vein of violet here and there amongst them. I glanced at Wilfrid, not knowing what sort of mood this first glimpse of the yacht would put into him, but there was no alteration of face. His countenance had set into an iron hard expression;

methought resolution could never show more grimly stubborn. Miss Jennings came to the side to look.

'There is little to be seen as yet,' said I to her, 'but we shall be heaving her hull up very soon. She is taking it quietly.'

Finn stood near; I took his glass from him and levelled it. 'Why, 'tis merely *ambling* with her, captain,' said I; 'gaff topsails down and no hint of squaresail that I can make out. The cloud we are making astern should puzzle her. D'ye think Captain Fidler will recognise this vessel?'

'Why, yes, sir; bound to it,' he answered; 'we aren't like the "Shark," you know; our figure-head alone is as good as naming us. Then our sheer of bow 'ud sarve like a sign-post to Fidler. Back this by our square rig and he'd have to ha' fallen dark to mistake,' meaning by dark, blind.

'Is the "Shark" to be as easily recognised?' asked Miss Jennings, who stood close by me, occasionally laying her hand upon my arm to steady herself and putting the other to her lips to speak, for the breeze rang with a scream in it at times over the rail in a manner to sweep the words out of her mouth as though her syllables were the smoke of a cigarette. Finn shook his long head.

'Lay me close aboard, miss,' said he, 'and I'll tell you the "Shark" from another craft; but there's nothen distinct about her as there is with us. She's black without gilt like a great many others, of a slaving pattern, long, low, without spring forrads or aft, with apple sides like others again. But,' said he after a pause, during which he had taken a look through his telescope at the glistening fragment hovering like a butterfly over the bow, 'though I don't want to say too much, sir, I'd be willing to lay down a good bit o' money on the chance of yonder chap proving the "Shark." Time, place, all sarcumstances point her out.'

'True,' said I; 'but there are many schooners afloat.'

'Ay, sir; but such a coincidence as *that*, your honour,' said he, pointing, 'sits too far on the werge of what's likely to fit it to sarve as part of a man's reckonings.'

'I agree with Captain Finn,' said Miss Laura; 'besides, I feel *here* that it is the vessel we are pursuing.' She laid her hand upon her bosom and turned to cross the deck where her chair was.

I assisted her to her seat with a peep out of the corner of my eyes at Wilfrid, but there was no encouragement in his face; so, posting myself forward of the companion for the shelter of it, I lighted a cigar and puffed away in silence till the luncheon bell rang. Wilfrid did not come to table. When I returned on deck after lingering nearly an hour below, partly with the wish to put some heart into Miss Jennings, who was pitifully dejected and nervous, and partly because I had had a long spell in the open air and guessed that for some time yet there would be little enough of the schooner showing to be worth looking at—I say when I returned I found my cousin at the rail with his arms tightly clasped on his breast staring fixedly ahead, with a face grim, indeed, with the scowling contraction of the brows, but as collected in the determined severity of it as can be imagined. In fact, the sight of the schooner ahead had gathered all his faculties and wandering fancies and imaginations into a bunch, so to speak, and his mind as you saw it in his eyes, in the set of his lips, in the resolved and contained posture of his body, was as steady as that of the sanest man aboard us. It was without wonder, however, that I perceived we had risen the yacht to the line of her rail, when I noticed that she still kept under short canvas whilst the 'Bride' was bursting through the surges to the impulse now even of the lower studdingsail. I took Finn's glass from him and made out a very handsome schooner, loftily sparred, with an immense head to her mainsail, the boom of which hung far over her quarter, whilst she swang in graceful floating leapings from hollow to ridge with the round of her stern lifting black and flashing off each melting brow that underran her. We had, indeed, come up with her hand over hand, but then it would be almost the worst point of sailing for a fore-and aft vessel, whilst we were carrying in our square rig alone pretty nearly the same surface of canvas that she had abroad. She was too far off as yet, even with the aid of the glass, to distinguish her people.

'What do you think, Finn, *now?*' said I, turning to him. He stood close beside me with his long face working with anxiety, and straining his sight till I thought he would shoot his eyes out of their sockets.

'If she ain't the "Shark," said he, 'she's the "Flying Dutchman." I had but one doubt. Yonder craft's boats are white, and my notion, but I couldn't swear to him, was that the "Shark's" boats were blue. I've been forrards amongst the men, a few of whom are acquainted with Lord Winterton's yacht, and one of 'em says her boats was blue, whilst th' others are willing to bet their lives that they are white.'

'But the cut of her as she shows yonder proves her the "Shark," you think?

'I do, sir,' he answered emphatically.

'Well,' said I, fetching a deep breath, 'after *this* hang me if I don't burn my book and agree with your mate, old Jacob Crimp, to believe in ghosts.'

I levelled the glass again and uttered an exclamation as I got the lenses to bear upon her. 'By thunder, Finn! yes, they look to have the scent of us now. See! there goes her gaff top-sail!'

Wilfrid caught my words. 'What are they doing?' he roared, bursting out in a mad way from his rapt iron like silence; 'making sail, d'ye say?' and he came running up to us with an odd thrusting forward of his head as though straining to determine what was scarce more than a blur to his short sight. He snatched the glass from my hand. 'Yes,' he shouted, 'and there goes her squaresail. By every saint, Finn, there's an end of *my* doubts;' and he closed the glass with a ringing of the tubes as he telescoped them that would have made you think the thing was in pieces in his hands.

'Shall I signal her to heave to, your honour?' exclaimed Finn, speaking with a doubtful eye as if measuring the distance.

'Ay, at once,' cried Wilfrid, 'but'—he cast a

look at the gaff end—'she'll not see your colours there,' pointing vehemently.

I'll run 'em up at the fore, Sir Wilfrid; they'll blow out plain there with the t'gallant halliards let go.'

'Do as you will, only you must make her know my meaning,' cried my cousin, and he went with an impetuous stride right aft and resumed his former sentinel posture. Miss Jennings came timidly up to me.

'She is the "Shark," then?' she said in a low voice.

'All who know her are agreed, Finn says, saving here and there a doubt about the colour of her boats,' I answered.

She had a sailor's eye for sea effects, and instantly noticed that the schooner ahead had broadened her show of canvas.

'Do they suspect who we are?' she exclaimed, talking as though she were musing.

'No doubt the "Bride" is recognised, and they will run away if they can.'

She looked at Wilfrid. 'I do not like to speak to him,' she exclaimed.

'He's killing Hope-Kennedy over and over again, said I: 'his wife is before him too, and he is haranguing her. Bless us, what a wonderful thing human imagination is!'

Up went the signal flags forward in a string of balls, a man tugged, the bunting broke and streamed out in its variety of lustrous colours, every flag stiff as a sheet of horn handpainted, with the light of the sky past it showing through. I caught myself breathing short and hard whilst waiting for what was to follow this summons to the running craft. We had been crushing through it after her with the speed of a steamer, and, supposing her indeed to be the 'Shark,' had literally verified Wilfrid's boast that the 'Bride' could sail two feet to her one. But now that she had broadened her wings there was a threat of considerable tediousness in the chase.

'Do you suppose they have made out what yacht we are?' I asked Finn.

'Likely as not, sir. I shall think so for sartin if they don't shorten sail on reading that bunting up there. A stranger 'ud be willing enough to speak us. Why not? 'Tis understandable that Fidler should have kept his rags small in the face of the muck that was crawling in the nor'rad this morning. *He's* got nothen to chase, and was always a careful man, so I've heard, and I tell ye, sir,' said he in a subdued way, speaking with his eyes fixed on Miss Jennings, who stood close with a white face, 'that the sight of his easy canvas is almost the same to me as seeing of her ladyship a sitting there,' levelling his hairy finger at the yacht, 'for, fond as she was of the water, let anything of a breeze come and she was always for having Sir Wilfrid reduce sail.' He put the glass to his eye as he spoke. 'Hillo!' he exclaimed in an instant, 'they're hoisting a colour. There it goes—there it blows. Oh my precious eyes! What is it? what is it?' he rumbled, talking to himself and working into the glass as though he would drive an eye clean through it. 'Why, Mr. Monson,' he bawled, 'I'm Field Marshal the Duke o' Wellington, sir, if she han't hoisted Dutch colours.'

I snatched the glass from his hand, and sure enough made out the Batavian horizontal tricolour streaming from the peak signal halliards like a fragment of rainbow against the lustrous curve of the mainsail.

'Wilfrid,' I shouted, addressing him as he stood right aft, Miss Laura and I and the skipper being grouped a little forward of the main rigging, 'they've hoisted Dutch colours. She's a Hollander, not the "Shark!"' and I fetched something like a breath of relief, for it was a condition of suspense that you wanted to see an end to one fashion or another as quickly as possible.

He approached us slowly, took the glass from

my hand in silence and after a steady inspection turned to Finn.

'She's the "Shark,"' he said, with a fierce snap in his manner that was like letting fly a pistol at the skipper.

'Your honour thinks so?'

'Don't you?'

'Them Dutch colours, Sir Wilfrid——'

'A device, a trick! What could confirm one's suspicions more than yonder display of a foreign ensign? She's the "Shark," I tell you, and that colour's a stratagem. What do you say, Charles?'

'I'm blest if I know what to think,' said I. 'If she's the "Shark," why has she taken it so leisurely, only just now setting her squaresail and gaff topsail though we have been in sight for a long time, crowding down upon her under a press that should awhile since have excited their suspicions? No need for them to hoist Dutch colours. If Fidler thinks he is chased, why don't he haul his wind instead of keeping that fore-and-aft concern almost dead before it, as if he didn't know on which side to carry his main boom?'

'She's the "Shark"!' thundered Wilfrid; 'the flag she is flying is a lie. Finn,' he cried in a voice so savagely imperious, so confoundedly menacing, that I saw Miss Laura shrink, whilst the poor skipper gave a hop as though he had touched something red-hot; 'are we overhauling that vessel?'

'Yes, Sir Wilfrid.'

'How long will it take us to come within gun-shot of her?'

Finn scratched the back of his head. 'Mr. Monson, sir,' said he, addressing me, 'that gun 'll throw about three-quarters of a mile, I allow.'

'Call it a mile,' said I.

My cousin, with his nostrils distended to the widest, his respiration hysteric, his whole body on the move, and with that *raised* look in his face I have formerly described, stared at Finn as though he would slay him with his gaze. The skipper scratched the back of his head again.

'Well, your honour, if yon schooner holds as she is and this here breeze don't take off, we ought to be within gun-shot,' here he produced a silver watch of the size and shape of an apple, 'in three hours' time, making it about half-past five.'

'How far is she distant now?'

'Betwixt three and four mile, Sir Wilfrid.'

'Get your gun ready.'

'A blank shot, your honour?'

'A blank devil and be damned to you. Load with ball. Who's your gunner?'

'We shall have to manage amongst us, Sir Wilfrid,' turning a face of alarm upon me.

I was about to remonstrate, but there was an expression in the eye that my cousin bent on me at that instant that caused me to take Miss Jennings' hand as an invitation to her to cross the deck and walk.

'Charles,' said he, 'you told me that you knew something about gunnery. Will you handle that weapon yonder for me?'

'Wilf, it is madness,' said I. 'What! plump a shot into a craft that may not be the vessel you want! or, which in my opinion is just as bad, fire at with a chance of sinking a yacht with a lady aboard—that lady your wife—the woman whom you have embarked on this extraordinary adventure to rescue?'

My blood rose with my words. I dared not trust myself to reason with him. I crossed the deck with Miss Laura, and when we faced round I spied Wilfrid marching forwards with Finn, and presently he was by the side of the gun gesticulating vehemently to a body of seamen who had collected round the piece.

Our signals were kept flying at the fore, whilst with the naked eye one could behold the minute spot of colour steadfast at the schooner's peak. Onwards she held her course, swarming steadily forward in long gliding curtseyings over each frothing surge that chased her, a most shapely and beautiful figure with a long flash of her low black wet side coming off the line of foam like a lift of dull sunshine, whilst on high soared the stretches of her sails with something of the airiness of a dragon-fly's wing in the milk-white softness of their spaces against the cloudy distance beyond. The time passed, Wilfrid remained forward. He stood upon one of the anchors swaying with folded arms to the movement of the yacht, stiff as a handspike, his face fixedly directed at the schooner ahead. The sailors hung about, chewing hard, spitting much, saying things to one another past the hairy backs of their hands, here and there a whiskered face looking stupid with a sort of dull wonder that was like an inane smile; but the fact is, from Cutbill down to the youngest hand all the seamen were puzzled, excited and uneasy. The state of my cousin's mind showed plainly to the least penetrating of those nautical eyes. No man amongst them could imagine what wild directions would be delivered, and though I made no doubt the gun would be let fly when the order to fire was given, I was pretty sure that should it come to a command to board the schooner by force the men would decline. Sometimes Finn was forward, fluttering near Wilfrid, sometimes aft, restlessly inspecting the compass or going feverishly to the side and looking over, when again and again I would hear him say in a voice as harsh as the sound of a carpenter's plane, 'Glory, glory! blow, my sweet breeze, blow!' manifestly unconscious that he spoke aloud, but evidently obtaining some ease of mind from the ejaculation.

The sun went floating down westwards, the breeze shifted a point or two towards him and then slackened, though it continued to blow a fine sailing wind with a regular sea that had long before lost the early snappish and worrying hurl put into it by the first of the dark blast. Slowly we had been gaining upon the chase; minute after minute I had been expecting to see her put her helm down, flatten her sheets, and go staggering away into the reddening waters weltering and washing to the sky under the descending sun, on what she might know to be some best point of sailing. She kept her squaresail spread and the Dutch flag hoisted, and swung stubbornly ahead of us, making nothing of our signals which still continued to fly. Through Finn's glass I could distinguish the figures of a few seamen forward and a couple of men pacing the weather-side of the quarterdeck. Now and again a head would show at the rail as though watching us, but the suggestion I seemed to find in the general posture and air aboard the vessel was that of indifference, as though, in fact, we had long ago exhausted curiosity, and had been quitted as a spectacle for inboard jobs and the routine of such life as was led there.

'*Is* she the "Shark"?' I said to Finn.

'If she isn't,' said he, 'my eyes ain't mates, sir. It is but a question of the colour of the quarter-boats.'

'I see no name on the counter.'

'No, sir, the "Shark" has no name painted on her.'

'She's steered by a wheel,' said I.

'So is the "Shark," sir.'

'What do the men forward who know the "Shark" think now?' I asked.

'Two of 'em say that it ain't her; the rest that it is. But ne'er a man aboard has that knowledge of her that 'ud give him conscience enough to take an oath upon it. Glory, glory, there she walks! By the piper that played afore Moses in the woods, your honour, 'twill be the fairest sunrise that ever I see that lights up the end of this damned mess, begging your pardon, Mr. Monson, and yours, miss, I'm sure. Fact is, I feel all of a work inside me, like a brig's boom in a calm.'

'I am unable to hold the glass steady,' said Miss Laura. 'Mr. Monson, I see no signs of a lady on board. Do you, Captain Finn?'

'Not so much as the twinkle of a hinch of petticoat, miss; but if her ladyship's there, of course she'd keep below.'

'You know Captain Fidler,' said I.

'Very well, sir.'

'There are two figures walking that quarter-deck. Is one of them he?'

'It's too fur off, sir. I've been looking and looking, but it's too fur off, I say, sir. Mind!' he suddenly roared, 'they're a-going to fire,' and he rolled hurriedly forwards.

A moment or two after crash! went the gun. The blast broke in a dead shock upon the ear, and the smoke blew away over the lee-bow as red with the tincturing of the sun as a veil of vapour at the edge of the crimson moon. Miss Jennings shrieked. A long yearning gush of sea catching the 'Bride' fair on the quarter swung her for a breath or two so as to hide the schooner, then to her next yaw with Wilfrid still on the anchor bending forward in impetuous headlong pose and two or three sailors handling the gun and a crowd of men in the head staring their hardest, the chase swept into view afresh.

'Ha!' I shouted, 'she's heaving to.'

'Oh, Mr. Monson!' cried Miss Jennings, clasping her hands.

Instantly Finn fell to thundering out orders.

'In stun'sails! clew up the t'garnsail! down squares'l; down gaff tops'l!' Twenty such directions volleyed from him; in a trice the decks of the 'Bride' were as busy as an anthill; canvas rattled like musketry as it was hauled down; the strains of Cutbill's whistle shrilled high above the voices of the men, and a true ocean meaning came rolling into the commotion and clamour from the yeasty seething over the side, the singing of the wind past the ear, and the frisky motions of the yacht as she brought the sea on her bow heading, to Finn's yell to the man at the helm, to range to windward of the schooner that was now fast coming round with her squaresail descending, her main tack hoisting and her topsail withering with her head to the west.

Distance is mightily deceptive at sea. How far off the schooner was when they let drive at her from our forecastle I could not say. She was probably out of range; at all events she showed no damage as she came rounding to, away down upon the blue throbbing which had softened much within the hour, with a bronze gleam of sheathing, as she heeled over ere her canvas broke shivering in the eye of the wind, that wonderfully heightened the beauty of the long, low, black, most shapely hull, and the bland and elegant fabric of bright spar and radiant cloths shining white yet through the faint claret tinge in the atmosphere. Wilfrid came slowly aft, constantly looking at her as he walked. Under reduced canvas we swept down leisurely, sliding lightly upon the run of the surge that was now on the beam. I examined her carefully through the glass whilst Miss Laura stood by my side asking questions.

'Is she the "Shark"?'

'She may be. But such of her crew as I make out don't look to me to be English.'

'Can you distinguish any women on board?'

'Nothing approaching a woman. They mean to board us. They have a fine boat of a whaling pattern hanging to leeward, and there are sailors preparing to lower her. They are not Englishmen, I swear. I see a large fat man delivering orders apparently with sluggish gesticulations, which strike me as distinctly Dutch. How about her figure-head?' I continued, and I brought the glass to bear on the bows of the schooner. 'Ha!' I cried, and looked round.

Wilfrid was watching the schooner right aft, where he had stood during the greater part of the chase, his arms folded as before, the same iron-hard expression on his countenance. I called to him.

'What is the figure-head of the "Shark"?'

He started, and answered, 'I don't know. Ask Finn,' and so saying walked towards us.

The skipper was giving some instructions to Crimp on the other side of the deck.

'Captain Finn,' I called.

'Sir.'

'What's the "Shark's" figure-head?'

'A gold ball in a cup shaped like a lily, your honour.'

'Then, Wilfrid,' I cried, shoving the glass into his hands, 'your pursuit must carry you further afield yet, for that craft's figure-head is a white effigy, apparently a woman's head.'

His manner to the sudden, desperate surging of the disappointment in him fell in a breath into the old form of the craziness of his moods of excitement. He looked through the glass, and then roared out—

'Finn.'

The skipper came bundling over to us.

'That vessel is not the "Shark."'

'I've been afeared not, sir, I've been afeared not,' said Finn. 'Like as two eggs end on; but now she's drawed out—'tain't only the figure-head. She han't got the "Shark's" length of bowsprit.'

Wilfrid dashed the telescope down on to the deck. 'A fool's chase!' he exclaimed, scarcely intelligible for the way he spoke with his teeth set. 'Heavenly God, what a disappointment! But it should have been Monday, it should have been Monday,' and his gaze went in a scowling, wandering way from us to the schooner.

'I suppose you know,' said I to Finn, 'that they're standing by to lower a boat when we shall have come to a stand?'

'Ay, sir, I know it,' exclaimed Finn, who had picked up his telescope and was feeling over it in a nervous, broken-down manner as though he feared it was injured, but durst not look to make sure while Wilfrid stood nigh. 'I shall heave to to looard for their convenience,' and with that he walked aft to the wheel.

Wilfrid looked crushed with something absolutely lifeless in the dull leaden blank of his eyes. It was perhaps fortunate for us, if not for him, that this sudden prodigious blow of disappointment should have completed the sense of physical and mental exhaustion which inevitably attended the war of emotions that had been going on all day in his weak mind, otherwise heaven alone knows what miserable and painful display might have followed this failure of his expectations. I was much affected by his manner, and endeavoured to console him, but he motioned me to silence with a gesture of the hand, and seated himself on the skylight, where he remained with his arms folded and his eyes fixed on the deck, apparently heeding nothing that passed around him.

'He'll rally after a little,' said I to Miss Laura, who furtively watched him with eyes sad with the shadow of tears.

'It ought to have been the "Shark," Mr. Monson,' she exclaimed in a low voice. 'My cowardly heart all day has been praying otherwise; and now I would give ten years of my life that my sister were there—for *his* sake, for mine, and for yours too, that this wretched voyage of expectation and mistakes and superstitions—oh, and I do not know what else,' she added with a little toss of her arms like a wringing of her hands, 'might come to an end.'

The sailors forward were eyeing the vessel steadily as we approached her. By this time all hands were aware of the blunder that had been made, and one seemed to see a kind of suspense in the posture of the fellows, with a half grin in it, too, as though 'twas an incident to be as much laughed at as wondered at. The breeze continued to slacken, the seas were momentarily losing weight as they rolled, the gushing of the western crimson floated in the air like a delicate red smoke, with a heap of flame-coloured clouds resting broodingly upon the southern confines and the new moon over the sun, a wonder for the bright sharpness of its curve in such a hectic as she stood in. We ran down and hove to within easy hailing distance to leeward of the schooner, but it was plain that Mynheer had no notion of talking to us from over his rail. His fine large boat hung manned at the davits as we rounded to, with a gang of fellows at either fall, and no sooner was our way arrested than down slowly sank the six-oared fabric. The oars sparkled in the red light, and away she came for us.

'Charles,' called my cousin from the skylight. I went to him. 'I'm too ill to be worried,' said he; 'represent me, dear boy, will you? Get us out of this mess as best you can, and as quickly.'

He spoke faintly, and slightly staggered after he had risen. Miss Jennings seeing this, took his arm and together they went below.

I stood at the gangway along with friend Finn. 'Twas a ludicrous position to be in, and what excuses to make I knew not, unless it was to come to my explaining the full motive and meaning of our expedition—a sort of candour I did not like the idea of. In the stern-sheets of the approaching boat was the large fat man I had previously taken notice of on the schooner's quarterdeck. His face was as round as the moon, with a smudge of bristly yellow moustache under a bottle-shaped nose; his person was the completest pudding of a figure that can be imagined, as though forsooth a huge suit of clothes had been filled out with suet. He wore a blue cap with a shovel-shaped peak and a piece of gold lace on it going from one brass button to the other.

'That's not Fidler,' said I to Finn.

'Fidler!' he ejaculated, staring with all his might at the boat; 'there's twenty Fidlers in that man, your honour. Why Fidler's a mere rib, lean enough to shelter himself under the lee of a ropeyarn.'

The boat came fizzing alongside handsomely, and the fat man, watching his opportunity, planted himself upon the steps and rose like a whale to our deck, upon which he stepped. In a very phlegmatic, leisurely way he stood staring around him for a little out of a pair of small, greenish, expressionless eyes, and with a countenance that discovered no signs of any sort of emotion; then in the deepest voice I ever heard in a man, a tone that literally vibrated upon the ear like the low note of a church organ, he said in Dutch, 'Who speaks my language?'

I knew a few sentences in German, enough to enable me to understand his question, but by no means enough to converse with, even if the man spoke that tongue, so I said bluntly in English, 'No one, sir.'

He wheezed a bit, looking stolidly at me, and exclaimed, 'You are captain?'

I motioned to Finn.

'Vy you vire ot me?' he demanded, turning his fat, emotionless face upon the skipper.

Finn touched his cap. 'Heartily sorry, sir: 'twas all a blunder happening through our mistaking you for another craft. I'm very willing to 'pologise and do whatever's right.'

The Dutchman listened apathetically, then slowly bringing his fist of the shape, if not the hue, of a leg of beef to his vast spread of breast, he exclaimed in a voice even deeper than his former utterance, 'Vot I ask is, vy you vire ot me?'

Finn substantially repeated his former apology. The Dutchman gazed at him dully, with an expression of glassiness coming into his eyes.

'Vot schip dis?'

Finn answered with alacrity, 'The schooner-yacht "Bride," sir.'

'Zhe vight vor herr nation?' sending a lethargic glance at our masthead as if in search of a pennant.

'No, sir,' cried Finn, 'we're a pleasure vessel.'

'Dere is no var,' exclaimed the Dutchman, shaking his head, 'between mine coundry und yours.'

'Ho no, sir,' exclaimed Finn.

'Den I ask,' said the Dutchman in a voice like a trombone, 'vy you vire ot me?'

This promised no end. I hastily whispered to Finn, 'Leave him to me. Turn to quietly and trim sail and get way upon the vessel. He'll take no other hint, I fear.' Finn sneaked off. 'Pardon me, sir,' said I, 'you'll have heard from the captain that our firing at you was a blunder into which we were led by mistaking your ship. We desire to tender you our humble apology, which I trust you will see your way to accept without delay as we are very desirous of proceeding on our voyage.'

He looked at me with a motionless head and a face as vacant of human intelligence as a cloud, with its fat, its paleness, its Alp upon Alp of chin, then ponderously and slowly putting his hand into his breast he pulled out a great pocket-book and said, 'Vot dis schip's name?'

'The "Bridesmaid," said I.

He wrote down the word, wheezing laboriously.

'Your captain name?'

'Fidler,' I answered.

This he entered.

'Owner?'

'Colonel Hope-Kennedy.'

'Ow you shpell?'

I dictated, and he put down the letters as I delivered them.

'Where you vrom?'

'Limerick,' I answered.

'Ow you shpell?' He got the word, and then said, 'Vere you boun'?'

'To the Solomon Group,' I answered.

This I had to spell for him too. He wrote with such imperturbability, with such a ponderosity of phlegmatic manner in his posture, with such whale-like asthmatic wheezings broken only by the trembling notes of his deep, deep voice, that again and again I was nearly exploding with laughter, and indeed, had I caught anybody's eye but his I must certainly have whipped out with the merriment that was almost suffocating me. He slowly returned the note-book to his pocket and exclaimed, 'Goot. You hear more of dis,' and with that walked to the gangway.

'Pray forgive me,' said I, following him and speaking very courteously, 'will you kindly tell me the name of your ship?'

He regarded me with a kind of scowl as he hung an instant in the gangway—the only expression approaching intelligence that entered his face, and said, 'Malvina.'

'And pray where are you bound to, sir?'

'Curaçoa.'

'Are you the owner, sir?'

'Captain,' he responded with an emphatic nod, and so saying he put his foot on the ladder and entered his boat.

Five minutes later we were breaking the seas afresh, making a more southerly course than was needful by two points, that we might give as wide a berth as soon as possible to the Dutch schooner, that, at the time I went below to the summons of the dinner-bell, was sliding away west-south-west a league distant under every cloth that she had to hoist.

## CHAPTER XIX.

### A MYSTERIOUS VOICE.

THIS was an incident to give one a deal to think and talk about. Certainly little imaginable could be stranger than that we, being in chase of a fore-and-aft schooner yacht, should fall in with a vessel so resembling the object of our pursuit as to deceive the sight of men who professed to know the 'Shark' well. I should have been glad to ask the Dutchman about his craft, yet it was a matter of no moment whatever. The thing had happened, it was passing strange, and there was an end. Likely enough she was an English vessel purchased for some opulent trader in the island of Curaçoa, and on her way to that possession in charge of the porpoise who had honoured us with a visit. The incident signified only as a disappointment. All dinner time I had been fretting over it, for since sunrise I had been thinking of the vessel ahead as the 'Shark;' counted, in a sort of unreasoning, mechanical, silent way, upon capturing Lady Monson out of her, which, of course, would mean a shift of helm for us and home again.

Wilfrid bore the blow better than I had dared to expect. He made a good dinner, for which he had the excuse of having fasted since breakfast, and broke into a noisy roar of laughter out of the air of gloomy resentment with which he had arrived from his cabin on my describing the Dutchman, and repeating his questions and my answers. In short, his weak mind came to his rescue. With the schooner had vanished an inspiration of thought that had served his intellect as an anchor to ride by. His imagination was now fluent again, loose, draining here and there like water on the decks of a rolling ship; and though he spoke with vehement bitterness of his disappcintment, and with indignation and rage even of Finn's ignorance in pursuing a stranger throughout the day, he dwelt very briefly at a time on the subject. Indeed, his talk was just an aimless stride from one thing to another. If he recurred to the Dutch schooner, it was as if by mere chance; and, though the subject would blacken his mood, in a very short while he had passed on to other matters with a cleared face. Miss Laura afterwards said to me that the strain of the day had been too great for him, and that when the tension was relaxed the strings of the instrument of his mind dropped into slack fibres, out of which his reason could fiddle but very little music. Well, I could have wished it thus for everybody's sake. Better as it was than that he should have shrunk away scowling and hugging a dark mantle of madness to him, and exaggerated the abominably uncomfortable behaviour I had witnessed in him all day.

He arrived on deck after dinner to smoke a cigar, and whilst I sat with Miss Jennings—for it was a quiet night after the stormy blowing of the day, with a tropic tenderness of temperature in the sweet gushing of the southerly wind, the curl of moon gone, and the large stars trembling through the film of their own radiance like dew-drops in gossamer—I could hear my cousin chatting briskly near the wheel with Finn with intonations of voice that curiously proclaimed the variableness of his moods to the ear, sometimes speaking with heat, sometimes in a note of sullen expostulation, sometimes surprising the attention with a loud ha, ha that came floating back again to the deck in echoes out of the silent canvas, whilst Finn's deep sea-note rumbled a running commentary as the baronet talked.

'What do you think of this chase now?' said I to Miss Laura.

'I wish it were over,' she answered. 'I want to see my sister rescued from the wretch she has run away with, Mr. Monson, but this sort of approaching her recovery is dreadful.'

'It is worse than dreadful,' said I; 'it is tedious with the threat of a neat little tragical complication by-and-by—any day indeed—if Wilfrid doesn't stow that gun in his hold or heave it overboard. The Dutchman might very well have answered our shot had he mounted a piece or two or driven alongside and plied us, as they used to say, with small arms. Now one isn't here for *that* sort of thing, Miss Jennings.'

'No. Is there no way of losing the cannon?'

I laughed. 'If Wilfrid will reserve his fire until he is sure of the "Shark" instead of blazing away at the first craft that resembles her, the weapon might yet prove something to usefully serve his turn; for I doubt if anything will hinder the Colonel from cracking on when he catches sight of us, short of iron messages from the forecastle there. But we shall not meet with the "Shark" this side the Cape, if *there*.'

'I fear it will prove a long voyage,' said she, with the sparkle of the starlight in her eyes.

'You will be glad to return?'

'Not without my sister.'

'But shall you be willing, Miss Jennings, supposing us to arrive at Cape Town without falling in with the "Shark," to persevere in this very singular and unpromising sea quest?'

'I will remain with Wilfrid certainly,' she answered quietly. 'My duty is to help him in this search, and where he goes I shall go.'

'But he will be acting cruelly to carry you on from the Cape unless able to certainly tell where to find the fugitives, fixing the date too for that matter.'

'I see you will leave us at the Cape, Mr. Monson,' she exclaimed with an accent that could only come from the movement of the lips in a smile.

'Not unless I prevail upon you to accompany me home,' said I.

She shook her head lightly, but made no answer. Perhaps it was her silence that rendered me sensible of the unpremeditated significance of my speech. 'Well,' said I, lighting a second cigar, 'whilst you feel it your duty to stick to my cousin I shall feel it mine to stick to you. Not likely I should leave you alone with him. No.'

At that instant the harsh, surly voice of old Jacob Crimp hailed the skipper, who still stood aft talking with Wilfrid. All was in darkness forward; it was hard upon two bells; the canvas rose as elusive to the eye in its wanness as a dim light in windy gloom far out at sea, and the shadow of it plunged a dye as opaque as blindness into the obscurity from the mainmast to the forecastle rail, where the stars were sliding up and down like a dance of fire-flies to the quiet lift and fall of the close-hauled yacht upon the invisible folds brimming to her port bow.

'Capt'n,' sung out Crimp's melodious voice—plaintive as the notes of a knife upon a revolving grindstone—from the heart of the murkiness somewhere near the galley.

'Hallo!' answered Finn.

'Can I speak a word with ye?'

'Who is it wants me?'

'The mate.'

'Tell him to come aft,' Wilfrid bawled out. 'If there's anything wrong I must know it. Step aft, Crimp, step aft, d'ye hear?' he cried.

Old Jacob's stunted figure came out of the darkness and walked along to where Finn stood.

'What is the matter, I wonder?' said Miss Laura.

I cocked my ear, for there is something in a hail of this sort at sea on a dark night to put an alertness into one's instincts and nerves. Besides, there was no sounder snorer on board than old Jacob, and his merely coming up on deck during his watch below, though he should have stood mute as a ghost, was something to raise a little uneasy sense of expectation. His voice rumbled, but I could not hear what he said. Wilfrid shouted '*What* d'ye say?' with an expression of astonishment and incredulity. Finn laughed in a sneering way, whilst old Jacob again rumbled out with some sentence. Then my cousin bawled out 'Charles, Charles, come here, will you?'

'What the deuce is the matter *now*?' said I, and Miss Laura followed me as I went over to the group.

'Here's a nice pickle we're in, Charles,' cried Wilfrid. 'What think you? Crimp swears the yacht's haunted.'

'So she be,' said Crimp.

'Pity your mother didn't sell vinegar, Jacob, that you might have stayed at home to bottle it off,' exclaimed Finn. 'Haunted! That may do for the marines, but you won't get the sailors to believe it.'

'That's jist what they do then,' remarked Crimp. 'All the watch below have heard it and can't sleep in consequence.'

'Heard what?' I asked.

'The woice,' answered Jacob; 'the same as you and me heard t'other night.'

'Have *you* heard a voice, Charles?' exclaimed Wilfrid, suddenly fetching a deep breath.

'A mere fancy,' said I.

'Ye didn't like it anyhow,' said Crimp gruffly, as though speaking aside.

'For God's sake tell me about this voice, Charles,' cried Wilfrid, agitated all on a sudden and restless as a dog-vane, with the twitching of his figure and the shifting of his weight from one leg to another.

I related the incident, making light of it, and tried to persuade him that the mere circumstance of my having said nothing about it proved that I regarded it as a deceit of the hearing.

'Did you know of this, Laura?' said Wilfrid.

'As a joke only,' she answered.

'A joke,' cried he, breathing deep again. 'The voice sounded off the sea, hey? and two of you heard it? What did it say?' and I could see him by the starlight looking towards the starboard quarter in the direction whence the syllables had floated to us. 'What did it say?' he repeated.

'Why, that this here yacht was cussed,' rattled out Jacob defiantly, 'and dum me if I don't think she be now that the blooming corpse belonging to the wreck is a-jawing and a-threatening of all hands down in the forepeak.'

'What is this man talking about?' I exclaimed, believing that he must either be drunk or cracked.

'He's come aft to tell us, Mr. Monson,' answered Finn, 'that he and others of the watch below have been disturbed by a woice in the hold saying that there's a ghost aboard, and that the only way to get rid of him is to sail straight away home and end this woyage which, saving the lady's presence, it calls blarsted nonsense.'

I observed old Jacob's head vigorously nodding.

'*You've* heard the voice too, Charles?' said Wilfrid, flitting in short, agitated strides to and fro beside us.

'Mr. Monson heard it twice,' growled Jacob, 'off the wreck as well as off the quarter.'

'Speak when you're spoken to,' cried Finn. 'Why, spit me, Mr. Monson, if it ain't old Jacob's grandmother as has signed on instead of Crimp himself.'

'Look here,' said Crimp, 'let them what disbelieves step forrards and listen themselves.'

'Charles, inquire into this matter with Finn, will you?' exclaimed Wilfrid. 'I—I—' he stopped and passed his hand through Miss Jennings' arm, immediately afterwards saying with a short, nervous laugh, 'the sound of a supernatural voice would cost me a night's rest.'

'Come along, Finn,' said I. 'Come along, Crimp. If there be a ghost, as our friend here says, he must promptly be laid by the heels and despatched to the Red Sea.'

'What did'ee want to go and tell Sir Wilfrid about that woice you and Mr. Monson heard t'other night?' grumbled Finn, as we moved forwards into the darkness towards the forehatch.

'Cause it's true,' answered Crimp in his sullenest manner. ''Sides it's time to end this here galliwanting ramble, seems to me, if we're going to be talked to and cursed by sperrits.'

Finn made no answer. We arrived at the forehatch and descended. The 'Bride's' forecastle was a large one for a vessel of her size. On either hand abaft was a small cabin partially bulkheaded off from the sailors' sleeping-room, respectively occupied by Jacob Crimp and Cutbill. Whether the mate ate with the captain, whose berth was just forward of the one that had been occupied by Muffin, with access by means of a sliding door to a small living room through which he could pass into the forecastle, I cannot say. It was a rough scene to light upon after the elegance, glitter, and rich dyes of the fittings of our quarters aft, but the more picturesque for that quality as I found it now, at least on viewing the homely and coarse interior by the light of a small oil lamp of the shape of a block-tin coffee-pot with a greasy sort of flame coming out of the spout, and burning darkly into a corkscrew of smoke that wound hot and ill-flavoured to the upper deck. There were bunks for the seamen and two or three hammocks slung right forward; suits of oilskins hung by nails against the stanchions, and swung to the motion of the vessel like the bodies of suicides swayed by the wind. The deck was encumbered by sea-chests cleated or otherwise secured. Here and there glimmering through the twilight in a bunk I took notice of a little framed picture, a pipe rack, with other odds and ends, trifling home memorials, and the artless conveniences with which poor Jack equips himself. There were seamen lying in their beds, a vision of leathery noses forking up out of a hedge of whisker, with bright wide-awake eyes that made one think of glow-worms in a bird's nest; other equally hairy-faced figures in drawers and with naked feet, huge bare arms dark with moss and prickings in ink, sat with their legs over the edge of their bunks. It was with difficulty that I controlled my gravity when on casting a hurried glance round the forecastle on entering it my gaze lighted on the visage of Muffin, whose yellowness in the dull lamplight showed with the spectral hue of ashes. His bunk was well forward; his bare legs hung from the edge like a couple of broomsticks; his hands were clasped; his head slightly on one side; his posture one of alarm, amid which, however, there still lurked a native quality of valet-like sleekness with a suggestion of respectful apology for feeling nervous. Sweet as the 'Bride' was, no doubt, as a pleasure vessel compared with other craft of those times, the odour of this interior, improved as it was by the flaring snuff of the lamp, not to mention a decidedly warm night, was by no means of the most delicious. Added to this was the lift and fall of the yacht's bows which one felt here so strongly, that, coming fresh from the tender heavings of the after-deck, you would have imagined a lively head sea had sprung up on a sudden. That Muffin should have stood it astonished me. Sleeping as he did, right in the 'eyes,' he got the very full of the motion. Besides, such an atmosphere as this must needs prove the severer as a hardship after the luminous and flower-sweetened air of the cabin. Finn took a leisurely survey of the occupants of the bunks.

'Well, lads!' said he, 'what's the meaning of this here talk about a woice? Mr. Crimp's just come aft to tell me there's somewhat a-speaking under foot here.'

'That's right, sir,' remarked Cutbill, who stood bolt upright like a sentry in the entrance to his little berth. 'I beg your pardon, Mr. Monson, sir, but it's nigh hand the same sort o' speech as hailed us from the wreck.'

''Tis the *same*!' said a deep voice from one of the bunks.

'Rats!' quoth Finn contemptuously.

'Never yet met with the rat as could damn a man's eyes in English,' grunted Crimp.

'Nor in any other lingo, Mr. Crimp,' said a singular-looking seaman, whose face I had before taken notice of as resembling the skin of an over-ripe lemon. He lay on the small of his back blinking at us, and his countenance in that light, that was rendered confusing by the sliding of shadows to the swing of the yacht, made one think of a melon half buried in a blanket.

'Well, but see here, my lads,' exclaimed Finn in a voice of expostulation, 'what did this here woice say? *That's* what I want to know. What did it *say*, men?'

'I told 'ee,' growled Crimp.

But old Jacob's interpretation did not tally with that of the others. The sailors were generally agreed that the voice had exclaimed in effect that the yacht was cursed, and that their business was to make haste and sail her home; but some had apparently heard more than others, whilst a few again manifestly embellished, with a notion, perhaps, of making the most of it; but there could be no question whatever that human syllables, very plainly articulated, had sounded from out of the hold ; all hands were agreed as to *that*, and proof conclusive as to the sincerity of the men might have been found in the looks of them, one and all.

'Silence, now!' cried Finn; 'let's listen.'

We all strained our ears. Nothing broke the silence but the sulky wash of the sea outside, seething dully, the half-stifled respirations of the sailors, who found it difficult to control their hurricane lungs, and the familiar creaking noises breaking out in various parts of the fabric to her swayings. Impressed as I was by the agreement amongst the men—and I had come besides to this forecastle with the memory very fresh in me of the mysterious voices I had before heard—I could scarcely hold my face as I stood listening, with my eye glancing from one hairy countenance to another. The variety of the Jacks' postures, the knowing cock of a head here and there, the unwinking stare, the strained hearkening attitude, the illustration of superstitious emotions by expressions which were rendered grotesque by the swing of the lamp, the half-suffocated looks of some of the fellows who were trying to draw their breaths softly, formed a picture to appeal irresistibly to one's sense of the ridiculous.

Three minutes passed, it might have been hours, so long the time seemed.

'Seems it's done jawing, whatever it is,' said Finn.

We listened again.

'Tell 'ee it's rats, lads,' said Finn.

'As the cuss was meant for this 'ere craft,' exclaimed the deep voice that had before spoken, 'perhaps if her owner was to come below, the sperrit, if so be it's *that*, 'ud tarn to and talk out again.'

'Tell 'ee, its rats!' cried Finn scornfully.

'Rats!' exclaimed Crimp with great irritation, 'if that's all why don't Sir Wilfrid lay forrard and listen for hisself?'

'Won't he come?' said one of the men.

'Come! no,' rattled out Crimp, 'and why? 'Cause he knows it's the truth.'

'Well,' exclaimed Cutbill, 'speaking with all proper respect, seems to me that what's meat for the dawg ought to be meat for the man in the likes of such a humble-come-tumble out of the maintop into the main-hold sort o' job as this.'

There was now some grumbling. Crimp had enabled the men to guess that Wilfrid was afraid to enter the forecastle, and sundry sarcasms, with a mutinous touch in them, passed from bunk to bunk.

'Avast!' roared Finn; 'listen if he'll speak now.'

But no sound resembling a human syllable entered the stillness.

'It's rats, I tell 'ee,' shouted the skipper, making to go on deck. 'Come along, Mr. Monson. Blamed now if I believe that Jacob *is* the only grandmother as has signed articles for this here woyage.'

But as I followed him the exclamations I caught determined me on advising Wilfrid to come forward. He had left Miss Jennings standing alone at the rail and was walking swiftly here and there with an irritability of gesture that was a sure symptom in him of a troubled and active imagination. On catching sight of me as I emerged out of the blind shadow on the forward part of the yacht, he cried out eagerly, 'Well, what have you heard? Is it a voice, Charles?'

'There is nothing to hear,' I answered. 'Finn disrespectfully calls it rats.'

'What else, your honour?' exclaimed Finn, 'the squeaking of rats ain't unlike a sort o' language. Put the noise they make along with the straining of bulkheads and the like of such sounds and let the boiling be listened to by a parcel of ignorant sailors, and I allow ye'll get what might be tarmed a supernatural woice.'

Wilfrid burst into one of his great laughs, but immediately after said in a grave and hollow tone, 'But you, Charles, have before heard something preternatural in the shape of a hail off yonder quarter, and from the dead man you found on the wreck.'

'Fancy, mere fancy,' I said. 'Gracious mercy! am I making this voyage to carry home with me a belief in ghosts? But I wish you'd go into the forecastle with Finn, Wilfrid, and listen for yourself. Make your mind easy: there's nothing to be heard. A visit from you will pacify the men. They hold that you admit the truth of what they allege by declining to satisfy yourself by listening. Their temper is not of the sweetest. They should be soothed, I think, when it is to be so easily done.'

He hung in the wind and said in a hesitating way, 'What do you think, Finn?'

'Well, Sir Wilfrid, since, as Mr. Monson says, there's nothen to hear and nothen therefore to cause ye any agitation, I dorn't doubt that a wisit from you would please the sailors and calm down their minds. I'm bound to say they're oneasy, —yes, I'm bound to say that.'

'Come, then,' cried my cousin, and he strided impetuously into the darkness, followed by the skipper.

I gave Miss Laura my arm and we started on a little walk. The awning was furled and the dew everywhere sparkled like hoar frost. The quiet night wind sighed in the rigging, and the yacht, a point or two off her course, and every sheet flat aft, softly broke through the black quiet waters with dull puffs of phosphor at times sneaking by like the eyes of secret shapes risen close to the surface to survey us. The sheen of the binnacle light touched a portion of the figure of the fellow at the wheel, and threw him and a segment of the circle whose spokes he held, out upon the clear, fine, spangled dusk in phantasmal yellow outlines, dim as the impression left on the retina by an object when the eyelid is closed upon it. My fair companion and I talked of the incidents of the day. One thing was following another rapidly, I said. 'Twas like a magic-lantern show; scarcely had one picture faded out when something fresh was brightening in its room.

'What manner of sound could it be,' she asked, 'that the sailors have interpreted into cursings and dreadful warnings?'

'It was no fancy on *my* part anyway,' said I, 'let me put what face I will on it to Wilfrid. If what the men profess to hear be half as distinct as what *I* heard, there must be some kind of sorcery at work, I'll swear.'

I led her to the starboard quarter, where I had stood with Crimp, and repeated the story. The darkness gave my recital of the incident the complexion it wanted; a tremor passed through her hand into my arm. It was enough to make a very nightmare of the gloom, warm as it was with the dew-laden southerly breathing, and delicate too with the small fine light trembled into it by the stars, to think of a hail sounding out of it from a phantasm as shapeless as any dye of gloom upon the canvas of the night. Ten minutes passed; I then discerned the figures of Wilfrid and Finn coming aft. My cousin's deep breathing was audible when he was still at a distance.

'Well, what news?' I called cheerily.

Wilfrid drew close and exclaimed, 'It is true. I have heard it.'

'Ha!' said I, turning upon Finn.

'By all that is blue, then, Mr. Monson, sir,' exclaimed the worthy fellow, 'there *is* somewhat a-talking below.'

'What does it say?' asked Miss Jennings, showing herself all on a sudden thoroughly frightened.

'What I heard,' said Wilfrid in his most raven note, 'was this, "*The yacht is cursed. Sail her home! Sail her home!*"'

‘ ’Twas as plain, Mr. Monson, as his honour’s own voice,’ said Finn, in a profoundly despondent way.

‘ D’ye think, Finn,’ said I, ‘ that it is a trick played off upon the crew by some skylarking son of a gun forward ? ’

His head wagged against the stars. ‘ I wish I could believe it, sir. The woice was under foot. There’s nobody belonging to the ship there. There’s no man a-missing. ’Sides ’tain’t a human woice. Never could ha’ believed it.’ He pulled out his pocket-handkerchief and polished his brow.

‘ Well,’ I exclaimed, ‘ so long as the thing, whatever it be, keeps forward—the deuce of it is, I’ve heard such sounds myself twice. It can’t be fancy then. Yet, confound it all, Wilf, there can be nothing supernatural about it either. What is it ? Shall I explore the yacht forward ? Give me a lantern, and I’ll overhaul her to my own satisfaction anyway.’

‘ You may set us on fire,’ said Wilfrid ; ‘ let the matter rest for to-night. To-morrow, Finn, you can rummage the yacht.’ He started violently : ‘ *What* can it be though ? Are we veritably haunted by the ghost of the Portuguese ? ’ He tried to laugh, but the dryness of the utterance seemed to half choke him.

'Well, let us wait for daylight, as you say,' cried I.

'I am going below for some seltzer and brandy,' said Wilfrid. 'Finn, you may tell the steward to give the men a glass of grog apiece. What can it be?' he muttered, and his long figure then flitted to the companion, through which he vanished.

It was evident the thing had not yet had time to work in him. He was more astonished than terrified, but I guessed that superstition would soon be active in him, and that there was a bad night before him of feverish imaginings and restless wandering. I could not have guessed how frightened Miss Jennings was until I conducted her below, shortly after Wilfrid had left the deck, where I was able to observe her scared white face, the bewildered expression in her eyes and a dryness of her cherry under-lip, that kept her biting upon it. Her maid shared her berth, and I was mighty thankful to feel that the sweet creature had a companion. Indeed, had she been alone, one might have wagered she would not have gone to bed that night. My cousin drank freely, but for all that a gloom of spirits settled upon him as slowly and surely as a fog thickens out the atmosphere and darkens down upon the view. He talked with heat and excitement of the strange voice at the first going off, but after a little he grew morose, absent-minded, with symptoms of temper that made me extremely weary, and I fetched a breath with a positive sigh of relief when he abruptly rose, bade us brusquely good-night, and went in long, melodramatic strides to his cabin.

I did my best to inspirit Miss Jennings, but I was not very successful. It may be that I was more half-hearted in my manner of going to work than I was conscious of. It never could come to my telling her more than that we might be quite sure, if we could only solve the mystery of the sounds which had frightened all hands forward, and aft, too, for the matter of that, we should be heartily ashamed of our fears in the face of the abject commonplace of the disclosure. She shook her head.

'It might be as you say,' she said, 'but if this strange voice continues to be heard, indeed should it not speak again and yet remain unriddled, what shall we think? I am frightened, I own it. I do not believe in spirits, Mr. Monson, in haunting shadows, and other inventions of old nurses; but I cannot forget that *you* have heard such a voice as this twice—you who are so—so——'

'Stupid,' said I.

'Matter of fact, Mr. Monson.'

But talking about the thing was not going to help her nerves. She went to bed at ten o'clock, and feeling too sleepy for a yarn with Finn I withdrew to my cabin. I found myself a bit restless, however, when I came to put my head upon the pillow, and would catch myself listening, and sometimes I fancied I could hear a faint sound as of a person talking in a low voice. Then it was I would curse myself for a fool and turn angrily in my bed. Yet for all that, I would fall a-listening again. It was quiet weather still, as it had been since sundown. In the blackness of my cabin I could see a bright star sliding up and down the ebony of the glass of the scuttle, with a pause at intervals, when it would beam steadfastly and intelligently upon me as though it were a human eye. Now and again the water went away from the side in a stifled sob. I could have prayed for such another squall as I have described to burst upon us for the life that would come to the spirit out of the lightning flash, the roar of thunder, the shriek of wind, the fierce blow of the black surge, and the tempestuous hiss of its dissolving spume. I cudgelled my wits for a solution of the voice, but to no purpose. It was ridiculous to suppose that a man lay hidden below. For what sailor of the crew but would not be quickly missed? And then again I had but to consider, to understand what I had not thought of on deck, I mean that even if a pair of hurricane lungs were secreted in the hold it was scarce conceivable that their utmost volume of sound could penetrate through the thick, well-caulked planking of the forecastle deck.

At last I fell asleep.

## CHAPTER XX.

### MUFFIN IS PUNISHED.

It was seven o'clock when I awoke. I at once rose, bathed, and went on deck, thinking, as I passed through the cabin and observed the brilliant effect of the sunshine streaming through porthole and skylight in rippling silver upon the shining bulkheads, the radiant lamps, the mirrors, rich carpet and elegant draperies of the cabin, what a very insignificant figure a night-fear cuts by daylight. The wind was north-east, a merry shining morning with a wide blue heaven full of liquid lustre softened by many small white clouds blowing into the south-west, and rich as prisms with the rainbow lights that kindled in their skirts as they sailed past the sun. The firm line of the ocean went round the sky tenantless. The yacht was making good way, running smoothly over the crisping and crackling waters under an airy spread of studdingsail which trembled a light into the water far beyond her side. Finn was on deck standing aft with his back upon the companion. I walked leisurely over to him with vitality in the very last recesses of my being stirred by the exquisite sweetness and freshness of the long, pure sunlit gushing of the wind.

'Good morning, Captain Finn.' He turned and touched his cap. 'How long is this delicious weather going to last, I wonder? Nothing in sight, eh? Bless us, captain, when are we going to run the "Shark" into view?'

He looked at me with a curious expression which his smile, that was always in the middle of his face, rendered exceedingly odd, and said, 'Did ye hear anything like a mysterious woice, sir, last night after you'd turned in?'

'I was for fancying,' I answered, 'that the atmosphere crawled with indistinguishable whispers. But I suppose without imagination there would be no lunatic asylums.'

He said, still preserving his odd look, 'The sperrit's discovered, sir.'

'Gammon!' I exclaimed.

'Ay! we've got hold of the woice!' he cried gleefully. 'Did ye ever see a ghost, Mr. Monson, sir? Look! *There's* the corpse as belonged to the wreck, and *there's* the happarition as was a cursing of this yacht last night in the forepeak, and your honour may take it that *there* is the invisible shape whose hail from off yon quarter has given old Jacob the blues;' and all the time that he spoke he was pointing to the fore-rigging just under the cross-trees.

I had before lightly glanced at a man up there, but had given him no heed whatever, as I supposed him to be a sailor at work. But now I looked again, shading my eyes.

'Muffin!' I cried with a gasp of astonishment. 'Do you mean to say——?' and I veritably staggered as the full truth and absurdity of the thing rushed upon me.

He hung in the rigging facing seawards, and there was turn upon turn of rope round his arms and legs; indeed he was as snugly secured to the shrouds as if he had been a sample of chafing gear. The sailors had compassionately jammed his hat down on his head, and in the shadow of the brim of it his face looked of the sickly yellow hue of tallow. But he was too high to enable me to witness the expression he wore. He had nothing on but his shirt and a pair of grimy duck trousers rolled to above his knees.

'What do you think of him as a sperrit, sir?' cried Finn, with a loud hoarse laugh which caused the sailors at work forward to look up grinning at Muffin, who hung as motionless in the shrouds as if he lay in a faint there.

'How long has he been seized aloft?' said I, with something of a pang coming to me out of the sight of him, for there followed close on my first emotion of astonishment a sort of admiration for the cutlandish genius of the creature that worked in me like a feeling of pity.

'Since dawn,' answered Finn. 'The men put him where he is. I let 'em have their way. I was afeered they might have used him in an uglier fashion, sir. Jack don't like to be made a fool of, your honour. Old Jacob, I'm told, felt bloodthirsty. Ye see, ye can't take a view of them sailors, specially such a chap as Cutbill, and think of 'em as lambs.'

'He must be an amazingly clever ventriloquist, though,' said I. 'Of course! All's as clear as daylight now. He was leaning over the rail when Crimp and I were talking on that night we heard the voice. I caught sight of him in the cabin a minute after the cry had sounded. The dexterous rogue! he must have sneaked with amazing swiftness below. A consummate actor, indeed! How was he discovered?'

'Why,' answered Finn, with a slow shake of laughter, 'there's a chap named Harry Blake, as occupies the bunk just over him. Blake, like O'Connor, is an Irishman, with a skin as curdles to the thought of a ghost. He was more frightened than any other man forrards, and lay awake listening. Time passed: all the watch was snoring saving this here Blake. On a sudden he hears the woice. He sits up, all of a muck o' sweat. Why, thinks he, it's the mute as lies under me a-talking in his sleep! He drops on to the deck and looks at Muffin, who presently fell a-talking again in his sleep, using the hidentical words that Sir Wilfrid had heard, and the tone o' woice was the same, sort o' muffled and dim-like; but it wasn't pitched fit to make a scare, seeing, of course, that the hartist was unconscious. On this Blake sings out, kicks up a reg'lar hullabaloo, tells the men that the woice was a trick of Muffin's. Muffin being half-dazed and terrified by the sailors crowding round his berth, threatening of him, confesses and says that he did it with the notion of terrifying Sir Wilfrid into returning home, as his life had growed a burden. The men then called a council to settle what should be done with him, and it ended when daybreak come in their seizing him up aloft as ye see there, where they mean to keep him until I've consulted with Sir Wilfrid as to the sort of punishment the chap merits.'

'What shall you propose, Captain Finn?' said I, with a glance at the bound figure, whose motionlessness made him seem lifeless, and whose posture, therefore, was not a little appealing.

'Sir,' answered Finn, 'I shall recommend his honour to leave it to the men.'

'But they may hang him?'

'No; I'll see they stop short of that. But, Mr. Monson, sir, begging your pardon, I'm sure you'll allow with me that Muffin 'll desarve all he's likely to get. Speaking as master of this wessel, I say that if he hadn't been found out in good time it might have gone blazing hard with all of us. The men were saucy enough last night, growling indeed as if it was next door to a mutiny being under way; and yet it was the first time of the woice speaking in the hold. Imagine it going on for several nights! It was bound to end in all hands giving up unless we shifted our helm for home, which Sir Wilfrid would never have consented to; so there ye'd have had a quandary as bad as if the sailors had been laid low with pison, or as if the "Bride" had turned to and leaked at every butt end. Then think of his anointing his honour's cabin with flaming letters; all to sarve his own measly wish to git out of an ondertaking that he don't relish. . . Mr. Monson, sir, he wants a lesson, something arter the whipping and pickling business o' my father's day, and sooner than that he should miss of his desarts by striving to get to windward of the soft side of his honour's nature, I'm damned,' said he, striking his open hand with his clenched fist, 'if I wouldn't up and tell Sir Wilfrid myself that it was that there Muffin as wrote the shining words about his honour's baby.'

'Best not do that,' said I. 'We want no tragedies aboard us, Finn. However, you may count upon my not interfering; but for God's sake let there be no brutality.'

'That 'll be all right, sir,' answered the skipper, with such a look, however, at the helpless and stirless figure in the rigging as satisfied me that his inclination, at present at all events, was not towards mercy.

It was not a sort of sight to make the deck a pleasant lounge till breakfast time. I was moved by some compassion for the unfortunate creature, mainly due, I believe, to a secret admiration for his remarkable skill and dramatic cunning; and understanding that the sooner Wilfrid was apprised of this business the sooner would Muffin be brought down out of the shrouds, I stepped below. The head steward came out of my cousin's cabin as I approached the door.

'Is Sir Wilfrid getting up?' said I.

'I've just taken him his hot water, sir. He

isn't out of bed yet. He's very heavy; had a bad night, I've been told, sir——'

I passed on and knocked.

'What is it?' cried Wilfrid, in a drowsy irritable voice.

I entered, and said, 'Sorry to disturb you, Wilf, but there's news that will interest you.'

He started up; 'The "Shark"?' he cried.

'No,' I answered, 'they've found out who talked like a ghost last night; who it was that whispered off the ocean to Crimp and me that this yacht was cursed; and who it was that made the corpse on the wreck hail us.'

He sat bolt upright with eyes and nostrils large with excitement. 'Who?'

'Muffin,' said I.

'Muffin,' he shouted; 'what d'ye mean, Charles?'

'Why, the fellow's a ventriloquist, an incomparable artist, I should say, to deceive us all so atrociously well.'

He stared at me with a face of dumb astonishment. 'What was his motive, think you?' he asked presently.

'He's pining to get home,' I replied; 'he's capable of any tricks to achieve that end. The men mean to punish him, and Finn is waiting to confer with you on the subject. They've had him lashed to the rigging aloft since daybreak.'

'The scoundrel!' he cried, springing on to the deck with a dark look of rage, yet with an indescribable note of relief as of a mind suddenly eased, softening the first harshness and temper of his voice. 'I have to thank him for a frightful night. What a fool I am,' he cried, vehemently striking his forehead, 'to suffer myself to be terrified by things which I ought to know—which I *ought* to know,' he repeated with passionate emphasis, 'cannot be as they seem.'

'Well, Wilf,' said I, 'you will find Finn on deck. He will tell you all about it, and you will leave the fellow's punishment to the men, or settle with Finn the sort of discipline the man deserves, as you shall think proper. I wash my hands of the affair, satisfied with Finn's promise that there shall be no brutality.' With which I left him and returned to my cabin, where I lay reading till the breakfast bell rang.

Miss Jennings was alone in the cabin. She stood with head inclined over some flowers which still bloomed in the mould in which they had been brought from England. The sunshine of her hair blended with the pinks and whites of the petals, and the gems on her hands trembled like dewdrops on the leaves of the plants as she lightly touched them with fingers half caressing, half adjusting. Her look of astonishment when I told her that the voice we had heard was a trick of Muffin's was like a view of her beauty in a new light; amazement with a sparkle as of laughter behind it to throw out the expression, rounded her eyes and deepened their hue. Then the little creature clasped her hands with gratitude that the thing should have been discovered.

'Muffin is quite a rascal,' she said, 'and so clever as to be a real danger.' She could scarcely credit that he had skill enough to deceive the ear as he had.

Wilfrid was slow in coming; I could see him through the skylight walking with Finn, gesticulating much, with a frequent look in the direction where, as I might gather, Master Muffin still hung. He kept Miss Laura and me waiting for nearly a quarter of an hour, during which I explained how Muffin had been discovered, how Wilfrid had gone on deck to arrange a punishment for him, and the like. Presently my cousin arrived, and on catching sight of Miss Jennings, cried out in his most boyish manner, 'Only think, my dear, that our superstitious alarms last night should be owing to a trick, but a deuced clever trick, of that illiterate, yellow-faced, tearful, half-cracked son of a greengrocer—Muffin. I never could have believed he had it in him. Eh, Charles? Mad, of course; I don't say dangerously so, but warped, you know, or is it likely that he would practise so cruel and dangerous a deceit merely because he wants to get home? Why, d'ye know, Charles, Finn gravely swears that, had the rascal persisted successfully for two or three nights, the yacht would have been in an uproar of mutiny, perhaps seized, ay, actually seized, through the terror of the crew, and sailed home—ending all my hopes.'

'How is he to be served?'

'Finn proposes,' he answered, 'that the men should form a court—a judge and jury. Their decision will be brought aft for our approval. If the sentence be a reasonable one, the fellows will be allowed to execute it.'

Miss Jennings looked scared.

'They won't hurt him much,' said I. 'Finn has pledged his word to me. 'Tis the fright that will do him good. Is he out of the rigging, Wilf?'

'Probably by this time,' he answered. 'I told Finn to get him sent down and fed. The sun is hot up there, and the poor devil faced it.'

Whilst we breakfasted I had much to say about the fellow's singular accomplishment as a ventriloquist; suggested that by-and-by he should be brought aft to entertain us, and expressed wonder that a man so gifted, qualified by nature, moreover, to dress up his singular and special faculty with the airs of as theatrical a countenance as ever I had heard of, should be satisfied with the mean offices of a valet. But my flow of speech was presently checked by a change of mood in Wilfrid. His face darkened; he pushed his plate from him, and let fly at Muffin in language which would not have been wanting in profanity probably had Miss Jennings been absent.

'Do you remember those strange warnings that I received about my little one?' he cried, turning a wild eye upon me. 'After the gross deception of last night, who's to tell me that I might not have been made a fool of in that too?'

I shot a hurried glance of meaning and warning at Miss Jennings, and said carelessly, 'Depend upon it, we can never be the victims of more than our senses in this life.'

'Why should the creature have left me to go forward?' he shouted.

I touched my forehead with a smile. 'When you engaged this fellow,' said I, 'you supposed his brain healthy anyway. Now, my dear Wilf, the motive of this voyage supplies plenty of occupation to the mind, and there is excitement enough to be got out of it without the obligation of a lunatic to wait upon you.'

He burst into a laugh, without however a hint of merriment in it, and then fell silent and most uncomfortably moody. Shortly afterwards he went on deck.

'What'll they do to Muffin, Mr. Monson, do you think?' Miss Laura asked.

'I cannot imagine,' said I; 'they may duck him from the yard-arm, they may spreadeagle and refresh him with a few dozens; punish him they will. Finn is hot against him. He is quite right in suggesting that a few such experiences as that of last night might—indeed must—have ended in a perilous mutiny. Are you coming on deck?'

'No.'

'But it is a beautiful morning. The breeze is as sweet as milk, and the clouds as radiant as though the angels were blowing soap-bubbles.'

'I do not care; I shall remain in the cabin. Do you think I could witness a man being ducked or whipped? I should faint.'

'Well, I will go and view the spectacle, so as to be able to give you the story of it.'

She pouted, and cried, 'Wretched Muffin! Why did Wilfrid bring him? Lend me one of

Scott's novels, Mr. Monson. I cannot get on with that story about the nobility.'

I was not a little surprised, on passing through the companion hatch, to find that the first act of the drama was about to begin. The whole of the ship's company, with the exception of the man who was at the wheel, were assembled on the forecastle. Crimp and Finn stood together near the forerigging, looking on. One of the sailors, who I afterwards learned was Cutbill, had pinned a blanket over his shoulders to serve him as a robe, whilst on his head he wore a contrivance that might have been a pudding-bag, though what it really was I could not distinguish. He had covered his chin and cheeks with a quantity of oakum, and presented a very extraordinary appearance as he sat with a great air of dignity on the top of a small bread cask. Six sailors stood wing-like on either hand him, constituting the jury, as I supposed. Confronting Cutbill was Muffin between two brawny salts, each of whom held him by the arm. The valet made a most melancholy figure, and even at the distance of the quarterdeck I could see his naked yellow shanks, his breeches being turned above the knees, quivering and yielding, till I began to think that the two sailors held him, not as a prisoner, but to prevent him from tumbling down.

Wilfrid was swinging to and fro the quarter-deck with long flighty strides, taking an eager, probing, short-sighted stare at the crowd forward when he faced them, and then rounding to step aft with a grin on his face and his underlip working as though he talked.

'I'm glad to see Cutbill making a fool of himself,' said I. 'Jack's jinks are seldom dangerous when he introduces skylarking after the pattern of that fellow's make up. Shall we step forward and hear the trial, Wilf?'

'No,' said he, 'it would be undiguified. Every man to the end he belongs to aboard a ship. Finn is there to see all fair. Besides, Muffin might appeal to me or to you, and I mean that the sailors shall have their way with him, providing, of course, that they don't carry things too far.'

'Let's sit, then,' said I; 'your seven-league boots are too much for me this hot morning.'

He called to the steward to bring him his pipe, and we posted ourselves on the grating abaft the wheel. It was a very gem of a picture just then. The canvas rose spreading on high in clouds of soft whiteness so silver-like to the burning of the sun that viewed from a little distance I don't doubt they would have shone upon the eye with the sparkle of crystal or the richer gleam of a pearl-encrusted surface. The decks went forward pure as ivory, every shadow so sharp that it looked as though an artist had been at work upon the planks, counterfeiting the rigging and every curve of stirless cloth and all delicate interlacery of ratline and gear running crosswise. The sea sloped in dark blue summer undulations, light as the rise and fall of the breast of a sleeping girl, into the liquid azure upon the starboard bow, where the steam-white clouds were gathered in a huddle like a great flock of sheep waiting for the rest that were on their way there to join them. The crowd on the forecastle filled that part of the vessel with colour. It was the fuller of life for the coming and going of the shadows of the far-reaching studdingsails and the marble-like arch of the flowing squaresail on the many dyes of the tough knotted, bearded groups of faces with heads of hair and wiry whiskers ranging from the blackness of the rook's plumes to a pale straw colour, most of the beards wagging to the excited gnawing upon junks of tobacco standing high in the cheek-bones, with here a wrinkled grin, there a sour cast, all combining to a picture that I have but to close my eyes to witness bright and vivid again as though it were of yesterday.

The trial was very decorously conducted;

there were no jeers, no cries, no noise of any kind. I could hear the rumble of Cutbill's deep-sea notes, and once or twice Muffin's response, faint as the squeak of a rat deep down. Crimp was called as a witness, and declaimed a bit, but nothing reached me save the sulky rasp of his voice. The fooling did not last long. Cutbill got on top of his cask to address the jury, and I saw the fellow at the wheel near us shaking his sides at the preposterous figure of the man as he hugged his blanket to his heart, gravely nodding with his pudding-bag first to the six men on his left, then to the six men on his right, whilst he delivered his charge. When this was ended Captain Finn, with a look aft, sang out at the top of his voice, evidently that we should hear him:

'Now, my lads, you who constitute the jury, what's your vardict? Is the prisoner at the bar guilty or not guilty?'

'Guilty!' all twelve men roared out at once, on which Cutbill, still erect on his cask, passed judgment.

I strained my ear, but to no purpose. It was a monotonous rigmarole of a speech, and so long that I turned with a face of dismay to Wilfrid.

'I say, what are they going to do with him?

Why, Cutbill has said enough to include whipping, ducking, roasting, hanging, and quartering.'

'They only mean to frighten him,' he answered, looking anxious nevertheless.

The two men who grasped Muffin walked him into the head, faced him round, and stood on either hand him, still preserving their hold. Finn came aft, the men meanwhile hanging about in a body forward in a posture of waiting.

'Well, what is decided on?' cried Wilfrid eagerly and nervously.

Finn touched his cap. He tried to look grave, but secret enjoyment was very visible in the twinkle of his eye, spite of the portentous curve of his mouth and the long drop of his chops to his chin end.

'Your honour, the men's vardict is that the prisoner's to be cobbed and ducked.'

'Cobbed!' cried Wilfrid, whilst I exclaimed 'Ducked!' with a look at the fore yardarm that stood high above the sea.

'Every man'll give him a blow with a rope's end as he walks forrard,' explained Finn, 'and arterwards cool him with a bucket o' water apiece.'

Wilfrid's eyes came to mine.

'It will depend upon how hard every man hits,' said I; 'the ducking is innocent enough.

Yet I see nothing of cruelty in the sentence ; and really the fellow not only requires to be punished, but to be terrified as well.'

'The hands are waiting for me to tell 'em to begin, your honour,' said Finn with a glance forward. 'It'll make the punishment too severe to keep the poor devil a-waiting for it.'

'One moment,' exclaimed Wilfrid ; 'did he offer any excuses ?'

'Why, sir, he said he was egged on with the desire to return to his mother and get off the sea which disagrees with his insides and affects his hintellectuals. He says he meant no more harm than that. Don't believe he did, but it might have ended in some smothering trouble all the same. "I came as a walet," says he, "and here now am I," says he, "broke—just a ship's dog, a filthy scullion," says he, "when my true calling," says he, "is that of gentleman's gentleman."'

'But, confound him!' cried Wilfrid, 'it was he who left me ; I did not dismiss him. He went forward of his own will.'

'My dear Wilfrid, he is cracked,' said I.

'Get on, get on and make an end of this, now, Finn,' exclaimed Wilfrid with a little colour of temper in each cheek. 'I'm weary of the business, and want these decks cleared and quiet to the eye.'

The skipper promptly trudged forward, and sung out as he advanced. In a few moments most of the sailors had ranged themselves along the deck in a double line. Every man held a piece of rope in his hand—reef points they looked to me, though whether they had been cut for this special business or had been hunted for amidst raffle of the kind forward I cannot say. Meanwhile a couple of seamen handed buckets full of water along from a little pump in the head until every man had one at his feet. When these preparations were completed the brace of salts who had charge of Muffin suddenly whipped off his shirt, and laid bare his back, so that he stood in nothing but a pair of breeches, a very radish of a figure—his yellow anatomy glancing dully in the sunshine, whilst the ghastly pallor of his face was heightened yet by his plaster of coal-black hair just as his inward terror was accentuated by the corkscrew-like writhing of his lean legs, the convulsive twitching of his arms, and the dismal rolling of his dead black, lustreless eyes. It was impossible not to feel sorry for the wretched creature. One felt that he was entitled, by virtue of the remarkable gift he had displayed, to a discipline of a more dignified sort than he was now to be subjected to. I laughed out, however, when Cutbill formed a procession. Absurdity could not have gone beyond the figure the great whiskered tarpaulin cut in his blanket and the canvas bag that served him as headgear as, making a sign, he tragically entered the double line of men, beating with his hands that Muffin and his two supporters should keep time with his strides. When Muffin was brought to the aftermost end of the rank of seamen Cutbill seized him by the neck and forced him to give us a bow. The two sailors who had conducted him to this point then posted themselves with the others, each of them picking up a rope's end, whereupon Cutbill, twisting Muffin so as to force him to face the vessel's forecastle, took a couple of strides backwards, extending his arms under his blanket to hinder Muffin from running forwards.

'Lay on now!' he hoarsely bawled, and then whack! whack! whack! whack! sounded upon the unhappy Muffin's spine as rhythmically as the tapping of a land-crab's claws upon a polished floor. Every fellow administered his single blow with a will, one or two spitting on their hands before their turn came. The sufferer writhed pitifully to the very first stroke, and to the fourth howled out like a dog. The sight half sickened me, and yet I found myself laughing—though, I dare say, there was something of hysteric nervousness in my merriment—at the preposterous spectacle of the staggering, twitching, dodging, almost nude figure of Muffin, throwing out into strong relief the huge blanketed form of Cutbill, who, with arms extended, his head with its adornment of oakum nodding gravely from side to side as if bestowing approbation on each man for the blow he dealt, strode backwards on majestic legs, carefully turning out his toes as though he were giving Muffin a lesson in dancing, and sliding along the lines of knotted, hairy faces with the air of some court functionary marshalling the progress of royalty.

As the echo of the last whack rose hollowly off Muffin's back, the skin of which was unbroken, though it was barred with white lines that resembled flakes of peeled onion, Cutbill whirled him round again, choking the yell he was in the act of delivering into a moan, and ran him back to where he had first started. The ropes' ends were now dropped; every man seized his bucket, and as Muffin moved, slowly confronted as before by Cutbill, who barricaded the way with outstretched arms, striding backwards once again with Cape Horn graces, he received a deluge full in his face one after another till I thought the very breath would have been washed out of his body.

'Now cut down below and dry and clothe

yourself,' roared Finn, as the last bucket was emptied over the shivering creature, 'and the next time, my lad, ye try any of your pranks upon e'er a man aboard this wessel, whether he lives forward or whether he lives aft, we'll send ye aloft to that yardarm there with a rope round your neck.'

Cutbill whipped off his blanket and tore the oakum and cap off his head. In a few brief moments the decks resounded with the slapping of sailors swabbing up the wet; buckets were stowed away in their places, the rope's-ends collected, and in an incredibly short space of time all was as though no such incident as I have related had happened, the planks drying fast, some seamen aft spreading the awning, other fellows at their several jobs in the rigging or on deck, just a grin now and again passing amongst them, but no laughter and no talk, and the yacht softly pushing forwards under the increasing glory of the sun fast approaching his meridian.

'We shall hear no more of Muffin, I think,' said Wilfrid, showing nothing of the excitement I had expected to find in him.

'No,' said I, with a yawn, and sickened somewhat by the business that had just ended, 'but all this sort of business doesn't look like the errand that has brought us out on to the face of these broad waters.'

'Ay,' said he, 'but that errand was in jeopardy until this morning.'

He went to the rail and took a long thirsty look ahead. I waited thinking he meant to return. Instead he folded his arms and continued gazing, motionless, with eyes so intently fixed that I took a look too, conceiving that he beheld something to fix his attention. A strange expression of surprise entered his face, his brow lightened, an air of eagerness sharpened his visage. 'Twas as likely as not that he saw with his mind's eye what he craved to behold in reality, and that the vision a sudden craze had raised up before him was as actual to his tainted imagination as if it lay bright to all hands upon the sea-line. But I felt wearied to the heart, sick as from a sort of ground-swell of emotion, worried with sharper longings to make an end of this idle quest than had ever before visited me. The mere sight of Wilfrid's posture and face was enough to increase the fit of the blues upon me just then, and I quietly slipped below for such sunny influence as was to be got out of the presence of the sweet little woman in the cabin.

## CHAPTER XXI

### HEAVY WEATHER.

After this, for a good many days nothing in any degree noteworthy happened. It seemed, indeed, as though whatever little there was to alarm or divert during this extraordinary voyage had been packed into the beginning of it. Muffin lay ill of his back for two days in his bunk; but for Wilfrid, Finn would have had the poor devil up and about within an hour of drying and dressing himself. The skipper could not forgive that menace of mutiny which had been involved in the yellow-faced joker's effort to procure the shifting of the yacht's helm for home, and he would always refer privately to me with violent indignation to the valet's trick upon his master. But on Wilfrid's hearing that the man was in pain and that his nerves had been prostrated by the punishment, he ordered Finn to let him remain below until he was better or well. There was no more ventriloquism; the midnight silence of the forecastle was left unvexed by muffled imprecations. The sailors, when Muffin left his bunk, asked him to give them an entertainment, to which he replied by saying he would see them in a nameless place first. The request, indeed, maddened him. I gathered from sullen Crimp's sour version of the incident that Muffin shrieked at the men, shook his fist at them, his eyes started half out of his head, the foam gathered upon his lips, and he heaped curses and oaths of a nature so novel, so unimaginable, indeed, upon them, that the stoutest shrunk back from the screaming creature, believing him to be raving mad. However, he behaved himself very quietly on deck. I never caught him looking our way nor speaking, nor heard him again singing in a dog-watch in his woman's voice. Life grew so tedious that I should have been glad to see him aft again for the sake of his parts as a mimic and actor. I was certain the man would have contrived a very good entertainment for us night after night; but Wilfrid said no, angrily and obstinately once and for all, and so the subject dropped.

The north-east trades blew a fresh breeze and bowled us handsomely athwart the broad blue field of the Atlantic. The 'Bride' was a noble sailer when she had the chance, and some of our runs rose to three hundred miles in the twenty-four hours, with a hill of snow at either bow and the frothing surge of the trades chasing us, and a sensible increase of heat day after day in the loud and shrilling sweep of air and the glitter of flying-fish sparking on wings of gauze from the white and gold of our vessel's shearing passage. We had entered the tropics, but had met with no ship that we could speak. At times a sail shone, but always afar. The lookout aloft was as steadfast as the rising and sinking of the sun. Day after day the polished tube up there was sweeping the glass-like sapphire of the ocean boundary, steadily circling the firm line of it, sweeping from either quarter to ahead. But the cry of 'Sail ho!' delivered at long intervals never resulted in more than the disclosure of a rig of a very different pattern from what we were in pursuit of.

A settled gloom fell upon my cousin's spirits. He complained of sleeplessness; his appetite failed him, he talked but little, and his one subject was the 'Shark.' I would sometimes long for a startling incident to shake him out of the melancholy that sat darkly as the shadow of madness upon him. Miss Jennings tried hard to keep up her heart, but already I could see that the monotony of the voyage, coupled with an incessant strain of expectation, was proving too much for her. She had come to this strange quest taking my cousin's word for what was to happen. She had given Wilfrid's programme of hopes no consideration. We were bound to fall in with the 'Shark' at sea, or at the very worst to arrive at the Cape before her, and there lie in wait. She was finding out now that the ocean was the prodigious plain I had represented it for a pursuit of this kind, and that the journey had already grown infinitely tedious, though Table Bay lay some thousands of miles distant yet. Still she stuck to her guns manfully. Her heart would show in her eyes when she thought herself unobserved; but if ever I approached the subject, in conversing with her on the vagueness and vanity of this pursuit, she would tell me that it was idle to talk, that she had made up her mind, that she had cast in her lot with Wilfrid in this chase, and that whilst he continued to pursue his wife, no matter to what part of the world he might direct Finn to steer the vessel, she would remain at his side.

'Should I ever forgive myself, do you think, Mr. Monson,' she would argue, 'if after I had left him Wilfrid found Henrietta and she refused to return with him for lack, perhaps, of the influence I should be able to exert?'

'Ay, but do not you suppose too much?' I would answer. '*Perhaps* Wilfrid might fall in with his wife; *perhaps* she might decline to have anything to do with him; *perhaps* if you were present she might yield to your entreaties. As my sympathies are not so deeply concerned as yours, I am able possibly to take more practical views. The one staggering consideration with me is this: we arrive at Table Bay and find the 'Shark' has sailed and there is nobody to tell us where she has gone. Figure our outlook then!'

'But you are supposing too. The 'Shark' *may* arrive whilst we are lying in Table Bay. What then, Mr. Monson?'

It was idle talk, though to her 'what then?' I might have replied by another question: 'If Lady Monson, at Table Bay, should decline to allow her husband to carry her home in his yacht, *what then?*'

It must have fared hard with me, I think, but for this girl; for had I had during this journey no other companion than Wilfrid, likely as not it would have ended in my carrying 'a bee in my bonnet' for the rest of my days. Between us we managed to kill many tedious hours with cards, chess, chats, reading aloud, whilst Wilfrid lay hid in God knows what mysterious occupation in his cabin or paced the deck alone, austere, unapproachable, with an iron sneer on his lip and on his brow the scowl of a dark mood out of which you might have looked to see him burst into some wild, unreasoning piece of behaviour, some swearing fit, or insane soliloquy—one knew not what; only that the air of him held you restless with expectation of trouble in that way.

The night-time was the fairest part of this queer trip when we got under the tropic heights, with failing breezes, hot and moist, softly-running surges languidly gushing into a sheet-lightning of phosphoric froth, a full moon that at her meridian came near to the brilliance of sunrise, the planets large, trembling, and of heavenly beauty, a streak of dim fire in the dark water over the counter denoting the subtle, sneaking pursuit of some huge fish; and reflections of white stars like dim water-lilies riding the polished ebony heave when it ran foamless. Evening after evening on such nights as these would Miss Laura and I placidly step the deck together or sit watching the exquisite effects of moonlight on sail and cordage; or the rising of the luminary above the black rim of ocean, with the tremble of the water in its light as though the deep thrilled to the first kiss of the moonbeams gliding from one romantic fancy to another as tenderly as our keel floated over the long-drawn respirations of the deep.

Indeed, it would come sometimes to my thinking that if the 'Bride' were my yacht and Laura and I alone in her—with a crew to navigate the craft, to be sure—I should be very well satisfied to go on sailing about in this fashion in these latitudes, under those glorious stars and upon these warm and gentle seas, until she tired. In its serene moonlit moods the ocean possesses an incomparable and amazing magic of spiritualising. The veriest common-place glows into poetic beauty under the mysterious, vitalising, enriching influence. I have seen a girl whom no exaggerated courtesy could have pronounced comely by daylight, show like an angel on the deck of a yacht on a hushed and radiant night when the air has been brimming to the stars with the soft haze of moonlight, and when the sea has resembled a carpet of black silk softly waving. The moon is a witch, and her pencils of light are charged with magic qualities. In the soft golden effulgence my companion's face would sometimes grow phantasmal, a dream of girlish loveliness, the radiance of her hair and skin blending with the rich illusive light till I would sometimes think if I should glance away from her and then look again, I should find her fairy countenance melted—a romantic confession that tells the story of my heart! Yes, I was far gone; no need to deny it. Our association was intimate to a degree that no companionship ashore could approach. Wilfrid left us alone together for hour after hour, and there was nobody to intrude upon us. Finn clearly understood what was happening, and sour old Crimp was always careful to leave us one side of the deck to ourselves.

But there was now to happen a violent change: a transformation of peaceful, amorous conditions of the right kind to affright romance and to drive the spirit of poetry cowering out of sight.

We were in latitude about eight degrees north; the longitude I do not remember. The night had been very quiet but thick; here and there a star that was a mere lustreless blur in the void, and the water black and sluggish as liquid pitch without a gleam in it. The atmosphere had been so sultry that I could get no rest. The yacht dipped drearily from side to side, shaking thunder out of her canvas and sending a sound, like a low sobbing wail, off her sides into the midnight gloom. This prevented me from opening the scuttle, and I lay half stifled, occasionally driven on deck by a sense of suffocation, though it was like passing from one hot room to another in a Turkish bath. There was a barometer in the cabin just under the clock in the skylight; every time I quitted my berth I peeped at it, and every time I looked I observed that the mercury had settled somewhat, a very gradual but a very steady fall. That foul weather was at hand I could not doubt, but it was hard to imagine the character it would take down amongst these equatorial parallels, where one hardly looks for gales of wind or cyclonic outbursts, or the rushing tempest red with lightning of high latitudes; though every man who has crossed the Line will know that the ocean is as full of the unexpected thereabouts as in all other parts of the globe.

I somehow have a clearer recollection of that night than of the time that followed, or, indeed, of any other passage of hours during this queer sea ramble I am writing about. It was first the intolerable heat, then the unendurably monotonous lifeless rolling of the yacht, with its regular accompaniment of the yearning wash of recoiling waters, the ceaseless and irritating clicking of cabin doors upon their hooks, the idle beating of canvas above hollowly penetrating the deck with a muffled echo as of constant sullen explosions, the creaking and straining to right and to left and above and below, a hot smell of paint and varnish and upholstery mingled with some sort of indefinable marine odour; a kind of faint scent of rotting seaweed, such as will sometimes rise off the breast of the sluggish deep when stormy weather is at hand. I believe I drank not less than one dozen bottles of seltzer water in the small hours. I was half dead of thirst, and routed out the steward and obliged him to supply me with a plentiful stock of this refreshment. But the more I drank the hotter I got, and no shipwrecked eye ever more gratefully saluted the grey of dawn than did mine when, wakening from a half-hour of feverish sleep, I beheld the light of morning lying weak and lead-coloured on the glass of the porthole.

An uglier jumble of sky I never beheld when I sent my first look up at it from the companion-hatch. It was as though some hundreds and thousands of factory chimneys had been vomiting up their black fumes throughout the night, the bodies of vapour coming together over our mastheads and compacting there lumpishly amid the stagnant air with the livid thickenings dimming into dusky browns; and here and there a sallow lump of gloom of the kind of yellowish tinge to make one think of fire and thunder. The confines of this ghastly storm-laden pall drooped to the sea within three miles of the yacht, so that the horizon seemed within cannon-shot—a merging and mingling of stationary shadows whose stirlessness was rendered the more portentous by the sulky pease-soup coloured welter of the ocean washing into the shrouded distance and vanishing there. All hands were on the alert. What was to come Finn told me he could not tell, but he was ready for it. His maintopmast was struck, that is, sent down on deck; he had also sent down the topgallantyard. Every stitch of canvas was furled, saving the close reefed gaff-foresail and the reefed stay-foresail. Extra lashings secured everything that was moveable. Much to my satisfaction, I observed that he had struck the long gun forward down below. There was not a breath of wind as yet, and the yacht looked most forlorn and naked, as though indeed she were fresh from a furious tussle as she rolled, burying her sides upon the southerly swell that was growing heavier and heavier hour by hour.

We were at breakfast when the first of the wind took us. It came along moaning at first, with a small dying away, and then a longer wail as it poured hot as the breath of a furnace blast between our masts. This was followed by some five minutes of breathless calm, during which the yacht fell off into the trough again; then, having my eye upon a cabin-window, I bawled out, 'There it comes!' seeing the flying white line of it like a cloud of desert sand sweeping through the evening dusk, and before the words were well out of my mouth the yacht was down to it, bowed to her bulwark rail, every blessed article on the breakfast table fetching away with a hideous crash upon the deck, with the figures of the two stewards reeling to leeward, myself gripping the table, Wilfrid depending wholly for support upon his fixed chair, and Miss Jennings buoying herself off to windward upon her outstretched arms with her face white with consternation.

The uproar is not to be described. The voice of the gale bellowing through the gloom was a continuous note of thunder and trembled upon the ear for all the world as though it was the cannonading of some fierce electric storm. The boiling and hissing of the seas made one think of a sky full of water falling into the ocean. The yacht at the first going off was beaten down on to her broadside and lay motionless, the froth washing over the rail; and the horror of that posture of seemingly drowning prostration, together with the fears it put into one, was prodigiously increased by the heavy blows of seas smiting the round of the hull to windward and bursting over her in vast bodies of snow. But she was a noble sea boat, and was soon gallantly breasting the surge, but with a dance that rapidly grew wilder and wilder as the tempestuous music on high rang out more fiercely yet, until it became absolutely impossible to use one's legs. The sea rose as if by magic, and the slide of the hull down the liquid heights, which came roaring at her from a very smother of scud and vapour and flying spray, gave her such a heel that every recovery of her for the next buoyant upward flight was a miracle of resurrection in its way. The hatches were battened down, tarpaulins over the skylight, and as for some time the stewards were unable to light the lamp we remained seated in the cabin in a gloom so deep that we could scarcely discern one another's faces. Off the cabin deck rose a miserable jangling and clatter of broken crockery and glass and the like, rolling to and fro with the violent movements of the yacht. For a long while the stewards were rendered helpless. They swung by stanchions or held on grimly to seats, and it was indeed as much as their lives were worth to let go; for there were moments when the decks sloped like the steep roof of a house, promising a headlong fall to any one who relaxed his grip of a sort to break his neck or beat his brains out. At regular intervals the cabin portholes would turn blind to a thunderous rush of green sea, and those were moments, I vow, to drive a man on to his knees with full conviction that he would be giving up the ghost in a very little while; for to these darkening, glimmering, green delugings the cabin interior turned a dead black as though it were midnight; down lay the yacht to the mighty sweeping curl of water; a shock as of the discharge of heavy artillery trembled with a stunning effect right through her to the blows of the tons upon tons of water which burst over the rail to the height of the cross-trees, falling upon the resounding deck from that elevation with a crash that made one think of the fabric having struck, followed on by a distracting sound of seething as the deluge, flung from side to side, boiled between the bulwarks.

We had met with a few dustings before we fell in with this tempest, but nothing to season us for such an encounter as this. I made an effort after two hours of it to scramble on all-fours up the cabin ladder and to put my head out through one of the companion doors. Such was the power of the wind that to the first protrusion of my nose I felt as if my face had been cut off as by a knife and swept overboard. The hurricane was as hot as though charged with fire; the clouds of foam blown off the sea and whirling hoarily under the black vapour low down above our mastheads looked like steam boiling up off the hissing surface of the mighty ocean cauldron. I caught sight of a couple of fellows lashed to the wheel and the figure of Finn glittering in black oilskins crouching aft under the lee of the bulwark, swinging to a rope's end round his waist; but all forward was haze, storms of foam, a glimpse of the yacht's bows soaring black and streaming, then striking down madly into a very hell of white waters which leapt upwards to the smiting of the structure in marble-like columns, round, firm, brilliant, like the stem of a waterspout, but with heads which instantly vanished in a smoke of crystals before the shriek and thunder of the blast. The fragment of gaff foresail held bravely, dark with brine from peak to clew, with a furious salival draining of wet from the foot of it out of the hollow into which there was a ceaseless mad hurling of water.

Heaven preserve me! never could I have imagined such a sight as that sea presented. It might well have scared the heart of a far bolder man than ever I professed to be to witness the height and arching of the great liquid acclivities with their rage of boiling summits; the dusk of the atmosphere darkened yet by the flying rain of spume torn by the fingers of the storm out of the maddened waters; the ghastliness of the dissolving mountains of whiteness glaring out into the wet and leaden shadow; the leaping of the near horizon against the thick gloom that looked to whirl like a teetotum, mingling scud and foam and hurtling billow into a sickening confusion of phantasmal shapes, a mad, chaotic blending of vanishing and reappearing forms timed by the yell and hum of the gale sounding high above the crash of the breaking surge and the shattering of wave by wave as though in very truth it fetched an echo of its own deafening roaring out of the dark sky rushing low over this tremendous scene of commotion.

Whatever it might be that blew, whether a straight-lined hurricane or some wing of rotating storm, it lasted for three days; not, indeed, continuing the terrible severity with which it had set in, for we were all afterwards agreed that a few hours of the weight of tempest that had first sprung upon us must have beaten the yacht down to her grave by mere blows of green seas, let alone the addition of the incalculable pressure of the wind. The stay-foresail in one blast that caught the yacht when topping a sea was blown into rags, and whirled up into the dusk like smoke. A fragment of headsail was wanted, but whilst some men were clawing forwards to effect what was necessary the vessel shipped a sea that carried three of them overboard like chips of wood, leaving the fourth stranded in the scuppers as far aft as the gangway with his neck and both legs broken! We were but a small ship, and luxurious fittings counted for nothing in such a hellish tumblefication as that. Wilfrid kept his berth nearly the whole time, having slightly sprained his ankle, which topped by the motion prohibited him from extending his leg by so much as a single stride. On the other hand Miss Laura would not leave the cabin. I endeavoured to persuade her to take some rest in her bunk, but to no purpose. I did what I could to make her comfortable, crawled like a rat to her berth, where I found her maid half dead with fright and nausea, procured a pillow, rugs and so forth, got her over to the lee side, where there was not much risk of her rolling off the sofa, and snugged her to the best of my ability. I sat with her constantly, said what I could to keep her spirits up, procured food for her, fell asleep at her side holding her hand, saw to her maid, and in a word acted the part of a devoted lover. But heaven bless us, what a time it was! I would sometimes wonder whether if the 'Shark' met with this gale, she had seaworthiness enough to outlive it. Occasionally Finn would arrive haggard, streaming, the completest figure imaginable of a tempest-beaten man, and report of matters above; but I remember wishing him at the devil when he told us of the loss of the four men, for a more depressing piece of news could not have reached us at such a time, and Miss Laura's spirits seemed to utterly break down under it. It was impossible to light the galley fire, and we had to subsist upon the remains of past cookery and on tinned food. However, Finn told us that on the evening of the first day of the gale the cook had fallen and broken two fingers of his right hand: so that could a fire have been kindled there was no one to prepare a hot meal for us.

But a little before eleven o'clock on the night of the third day the gale broke. I was sitting alongside of Miss Jennings in the cabin, with a plate of biscuit and ham on my knee off which she and I were making a lover's meal, I popping little pieces into her mouth as she lay pillowed close against my arm, then taking a snack myself, then applying a flask of sherry to her lips and finding the wine transformed into nectar by her kiss of the silver mouth of the flask. A steward sat crouching in the corner of the cabin; the lamp burned dimly, for there had been some difficulty in obtaining oil for it and the mesh was therefore kept low. Suddenly, I witnessed a flash of yellow moonshine upon the porthole directly facing me, and with a shout of exultation I sprang to my feet, giving no heed to the plate that fell in a crash upon the deck, and crying out, 'Thank God, here's fine weather coming at last!' I made a spring to the companion steps and hauled myself up through the hatch.

It was a sight I would not have missed witnessing for much. The moon at that instant had swept into a clear space of indigo black heaven; her light flashed fair upon the vast desolation of swollen waters; every foaming head of sea glanced with an ivory whiteness that by contrast with the black welter upon which it broke showed with something of the glory of crystalline snow beheld in sunlight; the clouds had broken and were sailing across the sky in dense dark masses; it still blew violently, but there was a deep peculiar note in the roar of the wind aloft, which was assurance positive to a nautical ear that the strength of the gale was exhausted, just as in a humming-top the tone lowers and lowers yet as the thing slackens its revolutions. By one o'clock that morning it was no more than a moderate breeze with a high angry swell, of which, however, Finn made nothing; for after escorting Miss Jennings to her cabin I heard them making sail on deck; and when, having had a short chat with Wilfrid, who lay in his bunk earnestly thanking God that the weather had mended, I went on deck to take a last look round before turning in, I found the wind shifted to west-north-west and the 'Bride' swarming and plunging over the strong southerly swell under a whole mainsail, gaff foresail and jib, with hands sheeting home the square topsail, Crimp singing out in the waist, and Finn making a sailor's supper off a ship's biscuit in one hand and a cube of salt junk in the other by the light of the moon.

## CHAPTER XXII.

### THE ''LIZA ROBBINS.'

THE gale was followed by several days of true tropical weather: light airs before which our stem slided so softly as to leave the water unwrinkled; then pauses of utter stagnation with the horizon slowly waving in the roasting atmosphere as if it were some huge snake winding round and round the sea and our mastheads wriggling up into the brassy blue like the points of rotating corkscrews.

I rose one morning early, loathing the narrow frizzling confinement of my cabin, where the heat of the upper deck dwelt in the atmosphere with a sort of tingling, and where the wall, thick as the scantling was and cooled besides outside by the wash of the brine, felt to the hand warm as a glass newly rinsed in hot water. I went on deck and found myself in a cloudless day. The sun was a few degrees above the horizon and his wake flowed in a river of dazzling glory to the inverted image of the yacht reflected with mirror-like perfection in the clear, pale-blue profound over which she was imperceptibly stealing, fanned by a draught so tender that it scarcely lifted the airy space of topgallant sail whose foot arched like a curve of new moon from one topsail yard-arm to the other.

I had noticed the dim grey outline of what was apparently a huge shark off our quarter on the previous night, and went to the rail to see if the beast was still in sight; and I was overhanging the bulwark, sniffing with delight the fresh salt smell that floated up from alongside, scarce warmed as yet by the early sun, and viewing with admiration the lovely representation of the yacht's form in the water, with my own face looking up at me too, as though I lay a drowned man down there, when Finn suddenly called out: 'A lumpish looking craft, your honour; and I'm a lobster if I don't think by the stink in the air that her cargo's phosphate manure!'

I sprang erect, and on turning was greatly astonished to observe a barque of some four or five hundred tons approaching us just off the weather bow, and almost within hail. I instantly crossed the deck to get a better view of her. She was a round-bowed vessel, deep in the water, with a dirty white band broken by painted ports going the length of her, and she rolled as clumsily upon the light swell as if she were full of water. She had apparently lost her foretopgallant-mast, and the head of the topmast showed heavy with its cross-trees over the tall hoist of single topsail. A group of men stood on the forecastle viewing us, and now and again a head was thrust over the quarterdeck rail. But she was approaching us almost bow on, and her bulwarks being high, there was little to be seen of her decks.

'Very queer smell,' said I, tasting a sort of faint acid in the atmosphere, mingled with an odour of an earthy, mouldering kind, as though a current of air that had crept through some churchyard vault had stolen down upon us.

'Bones or bird-dung, sir; perhaps both. I recognise the smell; there's nicer perfumes a-going.'

'Has she signalled you?'

'Ay, sir; that she wanted to speak, and then hauled her colours down when she saw my answering pennant. She's been in sight since hard upon midnight. Crimp made her out agin the stars, and how we've stole together, blessed if I know, for all the air that's blowed since the middle watch wouldn't have weight enough to slant a butterfly off its course.'

'What do they want, I wonder?' said I;

'rather a novelty for *us* to be spoken, Finn, seeing that it has always been the other way about. Bless me! how hot it is! Pleasant to be a passenger aboard yonder craft under that sun there, if the aroma she breathes is warrant of the character of her cargo.'

A few minutes passed; the barque then shifting her helm slowly drew out, giving us a view of her length. As she did so she hauled up her main course and braced aback her fore-yards. This looked like business; for, had her intention been to hail us merely in passing, our joint rate of progress was so exceedingly slow as to render any manœuvring, such as heaving to, unnecessary. Finn and I were looking at her, waiting for the yacht to be hailed, when Crimp, who had been in the waist superintending the washing down of the decks—for he was in charge, though the captain had come up at once on hearing that there was a vessel close to us; sour old Crimp, I say, whom I had observed staring with a peculiar earnestness at the barque, came aft and said: 'Ain't this smell old bones?'

'Foul enough for 'un,' answered Finn.

'Dummed,' cried Crimp, gazing intently with his cross eyes whilst his mat of beard worked slowly to the action of his jaw upon a quid as though there were something behind it that wanted to get out, 'if I don't believe that there craft's the "'Liza Robbins."'

'Well, and what then?' demanded Finn.

'Why, if so, my brother's her skipper.'

Finn levelled his glass. He took a long look at the figure of a man who was standing on the barque's quarter, and who was manifestly pausing until the vessel should have closed a little more yet to hail us.

'Is your brother like you, Jacob?' he asked, bringing his eye from the telescope.

'Ay, werry image, only that his wision's straight. We're twins.'

'Then there ye are to the life!' cried Finn, bursting into a laugh and pointing to the barque's quarterdeck.

Crimp rested the glass on the rail and put his sour face to it. 'Yes,' he exclaimed, 'that's 'Arry, sure enough,' and without another word he returned to the waist and went on coolly directing the scrubbing and swabbing of the men.

'Mr. Monson,' said Finn, who had taken the glass from Crimp, and extending it to me as he spoke, 'just take a view of them figures on the fo'k'sle, sir, will 'ee? There's three of 'em stand ing alone close against the cathead. They ain't blue jackets, are they?'

But at that instant we were hailed, and I forgot Finn's request in listening to what was said.

'Schooner ahoy!'

'Hallo!' answered Finn.

'What schooner is that and where are you bound?' cried the man on the barque's quarter-deck in a voice whose sulky rasping note so exactly resembled Jacob Crimp's when he exerted his lungs, that I observed some of our sailors staring with astonishment, as though they imagined Muffin had gone to work again.

'The "Bride" of Southampton on a cruise,' responded Finn, adding in an aside to me: 'no use in singing out about the Cape of Good Hope, sir.'

There was a brief pause, then Finn bawled: 'What ship are you?'

'The "'Liza Robbins,"' was the answer, 'of and for Liverpool from Hitchaboo with a cargo of gewhany.'

'Thought so,' exclaimed Finn to me with a snuffle; 'd'ye smell it now, sir? How they can get men to sign for a woyage with such a cargo beats my going a-fishing.'

'Schooner ahoy!' now came from the barque again.

'Hallo?'

'I've got a lady and gent here,' roared the

figure through his hands which he held funnel wise to his mouth, 'as want to get aboard summat smelling a bit sweeter nor this. They was wrecked in a yacht like yourn, and I came across 'em in a open boat five days ago. Will'ee take 'em?'

'What was the name of the yacht, can you tell me?' cried Finn.

The man turned his head, evidently interrogating another, probably his mate, who stood a little behind him; then bringing his hands to his mouth afresh, he roared out 'The "Shark!"'

Finn slowly brought his long face to bear upon mine; his figure moving with it as though the whole of him were a piece of mechanism warranted to perform that motion but no more. 'Gracious thunder!' he exclaimed under his breath and then his jaw fell. I heard the confused humming of the men's voices forward, a swift flow of excited talk subdued into a sort of buzzing by their habits of shipboard discipline. I felt that I was as pale in the face as if I had received some violent shock.

'The "Shark!" I cried in a breathless way; 'the lady and gentleman then aboard that vessel must be the Colonel and Lady Monson. The yacht probably met with the gale that swept over us and foundered in it;' then pulling myself together with an effort, for amazement seemed to have sent all my wits adrift for a moment, I exclaimed, 'Hail the barque at once, Finn; say that you will be happy to receive the lady and gentleman. Ask the captain to come aboard, or stay—where is Crimp? Let old Jacob invite his brother. We must act with extreme wariness. My God, what an astounding confrontment!'

'Mr. Crimp,' roared Finn, on a sudden exploding, as it were, out of his state of petrifaction. Jacob came aft. 'Jump on that there rail, Mr. Crimp, and tell your brother who ye are and ask him aboard.'

The sour little man climbed on to the bulwarks, and in a voice that was the completest imaginable echo of that in which the fellow aboard the barque had hailed us, he shouted '’Arry ahoy!'

The other stood a while staring, dropping his head first on one side, then on the other, in the manner of one who discredits his sight and seeks to obtain a clearer view by dodging about for a true focus.

'Why, Jacob,' he presently sung out, 'is that you, brother?'

'Ay, come aboard, will ye, ’Arry?' answered Crimp, with which he dropped off the rail and trudged sourly to the gangway without the least visible expression of surprise or pleasure or emotion of any kind.

Meanwhile I had taken notice of strong manifestations of excitement amongst the little group on the forecastle of the barque—I mean the small knot of men to whom Finn had called my attention. The vessels lay so near together that postures and gestures were easily distinguishable. There could be no doubt now that the fellows had formed a portion of a yacht's crew. Their dress betokened it; they gazed with much probing and thrusting of their heads and elbowing of one another at our men, who lined the forward bulwarks—most of our sailors having turned up—as though seeking for familiar faces. I eagerly looked for signs of the Colonel and his companion, but it was still very early; they were doubtless in their cabins, and the crying out of voices from vessel to vessel was so recent that even if the couple had been disturbed by the noise they would not yet have had time to dress themselves and make their appearance on deck.

'Will you go and report to Sir Wilfrid, sir?' said Finn.

'At once,' I answered. 'Let old Jacob's brother have the full story, the whole truth, should he arrive before I return. His sympathies must be enlisted on Sir Wilfrid's side or there may happen a most worrisome difficulty if the Colonel refuses to leave that barque and should make some splendid offer to the skipper to retain him and her ladyship.'

'I'll talk with Jacob whilst his brother's a-coming, sir,' said Finn.

I stepped below with a beating heart. I was exceedingly agitated, could scarce bring my mind to accept the reality of what had happened, and I dreaded moreover the effect of the news upon my cousin. The 'Shark' foundered!—the couple we were in chase of picked up out of an open boat!—this great, blank, lidless eye of ocean whose infinite distances I had pointed into over and over again to Miss Laura yielding up the pair that we were in chase of in an encounter bewildering as a surprise and miraculous for its unexpectedness!—why, I confess I breathed in gasps as I thought of it all, making my way, absolutely trembling in my shoes, to Wilfrid's berth. I knocked and was told to enter. He had nearly finished dressing and looked up from a boot that he was buttoning with a cold, bitter, triumphant smile at me.

'I know,' he exclaimed in a voice infinitely more composed than I could have exerted; 'this is Monday, Charles.'

It *was* Monday as he said! I stared stupidly at him for a minute, and then saw how it was that he knew. The window of his port was unscrewed and lay wide open; through it I could see the barque fluctuating in the silver and blue of the atmosphere as she swayed, swinging her canvas in and out with every roll. The port made a very funnel for the ear as a vehicle of sound, for I could distinctly hear the orders given on board the vessel for lowering a boat; the voice of one of the 'Shark's' men apparently hailing our fellows; the beat of her cloths against the mast; and the recoil of the water breaking from her broad channels as she buried her plates to the height almost of those platforms.

'I am breathless with astonishment,' said I; 'but, God be praised, Wilf, I see you mean to confront this business coldly.'

'The captain of that vessel is coming on board,' he said, speaking with extraordinary composure, whilst his face, from which the smile had faded, still preserved the light or expression of its mingled triumph and bitterness.

'He will be here in a minute or two,' I answered.

'Is Laura up?'

'I do not know.'

'See that she gets the news, Charles, at once.

I shall want her on deck. Then return and we will concert a little programme.'

I quitted his cabin, marvelling exceedingly at his collectedness. But then I had noticed that his mind steadied in proportion as his attention grew fixed. This is true of most weak intelligences, I suppose ; if you want them to ride you must let go an anchor for them. I was hesitating at Miss Jennings' door, stretching my ear for the sound of her voice that I might know she was dressing and had her maid with her, when the handle was turned and the maid came out. I inquired if her mistress was rising. She answered, 'Yes.' 'Tell her,' said I, 'that there is a vessel close to us, and that Colonel Hope-Kennedy and Lady Monson are on board of her. Sir Wilfrid begs that she will make haste, as he desires her presence on deck as soon as possible.' I then returned to my cousin's berth, thinking that, though to be sure the news would immensely scare the little girl, it was best that she should have the whole truth at once, and so find time to tauten her nerves for what was to come.

As I entered my cousin's cabin I heard through the open port the sound of the grinding of oars betwixt thole pins, and immediately after there rang out a cry of 'Look out for the end of the line!' by which I knew that Crimp's brother was alongside of us. Wilfrid, having buttoned his boots, was now completely dressed. He stood with a hand upon the edge of his bunk, gazing at the barque, which still hung fair in the blue and gleaming disc of the porthole, showing in that circular frame like a daguerreotype with the silvery flashing and fading of light, the shooting prismatic tints, the shot-silk-like alternations of hues that accompanied the floating heave of her by the swell to the sunshine. I picked up a small binocular glass that lay on the table, but could see nothing as yet of Lady Monson or her companion.

'My wife was always a late riser,' said Wilfrid, turning to me with a haggard smile and a cold sarcastic note in his voice that was steadied, as your ear instinctively detected, by the iron resolution of his mood, as the spine stiffens the form.

'Had we not better go on deck?' said I. 'It might be useful to hear what the master of the barque has to say.'

'Inch by inch, Charles. There is no hurry. I have my man safe,' pointing at the vessel. 'Let us briefly debate a course of action—or rather, let me leave myself in your hands. We want no "scene," as women call it, or as little as possible. There are many grinning, merely curious spectators, and Lady Monson is still my wife. What do you advise?'

'First of all, my dear Wilfrid, what do you want?' I exclaimed, rather puzzled and not at all relishing the responsibility of offering suggestions. 'You intend, of course, that Lady Monson shall come on board the "Bride." But the Colonel?'

'Oh,' cried he sharply and fiercely, 'I shall want him here too!'

'Then you don't mean to separate them?'

'Yes, I do,' he answered; 'as effectually as a bullet can manage it for me.'

'Ha!' said I, and I was silent a little and then said: 'If I were you, I should leave Crimp's brother to sail away with the rascal. The separation will be as complete as——'

He silenced me with a passionate gesture, but said, nevertheless, calmly, 'I want them both on board my yacht.'

'Will they come if they are fetched, think you?'

He walked impatiently to the door. 'I must plan for myself, I see,' he exclaimed. He grasped the handle and turned to me with his hand still upon it. 'I see how it is with you, Charles,' he said almost gently; 'you object to my fighting Colonel Hope-Kennedy.'

'I do,' I answered. 'I object to this scoundrel being furnished with a chance of completing the injury he has done you by shooting you.'

He came to me, put his hand on my shoulder, bent his face close to mine, and said in a low voice, 'Do not fear for me; I shall kill him. As you value my love'—his tone faltered—'do not come by so much as a hair's breadth between me and my resolution to take his life. If he will not fight me on board my yacht, he shall fight me on yonder vessel. He is a soldier—a colonel; he will not refuse my challenge. Come, my programme is arranged; we are now wasting time.' He stepped from his berth and I followed him.

As I turned to ascend the companion steps, Wilfrid being in advance of me, mounting with impetuosity, I saw Miss Jennings come out of her berth. I waited for her. Her face was bloodless, yet I was glad to see something like resolution expressed in it.

'Is it true, Mr. Monson, that my sister is close to us in a ship?' she asked.

'She and the Colonel,' I answered; 'within eyeshot—that is to say, when they step on deck.'

She put her hand to her breast, and drew several short breaths.

'Pray take courage,' I said; 'it is for your sister to tremble—not you.'

'How has Wilfrid received this piece of extraordinary news?' she asked with a sort of panting in her way of speaking.

'He is as unmoved, I give you my word, as if he were of cast iron. You shall judge; he has preceded us.'

I took her hand and led her up the ladder. Crimp's brother had apparently just climbed over the yacht's side. As I made my appearance he was coming aft from the gangway in company with Finn and surly old Jacob. All three rumbled with talk at once as they made, with a deep sea roll, for Wilfrid, who was standing so as to keep the mainmast of the yacht between him and the barque. Miss Jennings started and stopped on seeing the vessel, that had closed us somewhat since she had first hove-to, so that it was almost possible now to distinguish the faces of her people. When my companion moved again she seemed to shrink—almost cower indeed, and passed to the right of me as though to hide herself. Then peeping past me at the vessel, she said, 'I see no lady on board.'

'Your sister is still below, I expect,' I answered.

She left me and clasped my cousin's arm, just saying, 'Oh, Wilfrid!' in a tearful, pitiful voice. He gazed down at her and pressed his hand upon hers with a look of dreadful grief entering his face swiftly as a blush suffuses a woman's cheek; but the expression passed quickly. Something he said in a whisper, then lightly freed his arm from her clasp and turned to the master of the barque.

'Captain Crimp, your honour,' said Finn, knuckling his forehead; 'Jacob's brother, Sir Wilfrid.'

Small need to mention *that*, I thought, for, saving that Jacob was the taller by an inch or two, whilst his brother's eyes looked straight at you, the twins were the most ludicrous, incomparable match that any lover of the uncommon could have desired to see; both of the same sulky cast of countenance, both of the exact same build, each wearing a light kind of beard similarly coloured.

'Yes, I'm Jacob's brother,' answered Captain Crimp. 'Heard he was out a yachtin', but didn't know the name of the wessel.'

'I'm very glad to have fallen in with you,' said Wilfrid, addressing him with a coolness that I saw astonished Finn, whilst Miss Laura glanced at me with an arching of her eyebrows as eloquent of amazement as if she had spoken her thoughts. 'I hear that you have a lady and gentleman on board your ship.'

'Ay,' answered Captain Crimp bluntly, though

somehow one found nothing offensive in his manner of speech; 'they want to leave me, and,' added he with a surly grin, 'I don't blame 'em. Gewhany ain't over choice as a smell, 'ticularly down here.'

'Their names are Colonel Hope-Kennedy and Lady Monson. Is that so?' demanded Wilfrid, speaking slowly and coldly.

Captain Crimp turned a stupid stare of wonder upon his brother, and then, addressing Wilfrid, exclaimed: 'Who tould 'ee? Ye've got the gent's name right: the lady's his missus—same name as 'tother's.' Wilfrid set his teeth.

I looked towards the barque, but there were no signs of the Colonel or her ladyship yet.

'The lady is my wife, Captain Crimp,' said Wilfrid.

'Ho, indeed,' responded the man, showing no surprise whatever.

'She has run away,' continued my cousin, 'with the gentleman you have on board your vessel, and we,' looking round upon us, 'are here in pursuit of them. We have met with them—very unexpectedly. It is likely when Colonel Hope-Kennedy discovers who we are that he may request you to trim your sails and proceed on your voyage home, and offer you a sum of money to convey Lady Monson and himself away from us. You will not do so!' he exclaimed with sudden temper, which he instantly subdued, though it darkened his face.

'I don't want no trouble,' answered Captain Crimp. 'The parties have been a-wanting to get out of my wessel pretty nigh ever since we fell in with them, and here's their chance. Only,' he added with a wooden look at his brother, 'if they don't choose to quit I can't chuck 'em overboard.'

'Oh yes, 'ee can, 'Arry,' said Jacob. 'What ye've got to do is to tell 'em they must *go*. No sogerin' in this business, 'Arry, so stand by. The law ain't a-going to let ye keep a lawful wife away from her wedded spouse when he tarns to and demands her of ye. Better chuck 'em overboard than have the lawyers fall foul of ye, 'Arry.'

This was a long speech for Jacob, who nodded several times at his brother with energy after delivering it.

'Well, and who wants to keep a wedded woman away from her lawful spouse, as ye calls it, Jacob?' exclaimed Captain Crimp. 'What I says is, if the parties refuses to leave I can't chuck 'em overboard.'

'See here, Captain,' said Finn, 'Jacob's right, and what you as a sensible man's got to do is to steer clear of quàndaries. His honour'll be sending for the lady and the gent, and you'll have to tell 'em to *go*, as Jacob says. If they refuse—but let 'em refuse first,' he continued with a look at Wilfrid.

'I don't want no trouble,' said Captain Crimp, 'and I ain't going to get in a mess for no man. Do what you think's proper. What I ask is to be left out of the boiling.'

As he spoke I touched Miss Jennings' arm. '*There they are!*' I whispered.

# CHAPTER XXIII.

## THE COLONEL AND HER LADYSHIP.

WILFRID saw them too in a flash. He slightly reeled, making a fierce grasp at some gear against the mainmast to steady himself. Distant as they were, one could see nevertheless that they were an uncommonly fine couple. A man who was apparently the mate of the barque stood near them, and, though seemingly above rather than below the average stature, he looked a very poor little fellow alongside the towering and commanding figure of the Colonel. I witnessed no gestures, no movements, nothing of any kind to denote astonishment or alarm in either of them. They stood stock still side by side, surveying us over an open rail that exposed their forms from their feet; he, so far as I could make out, attired in dark blue cloth or serge, and a cap with a naval peak, the top protected by a white cover; she in a dress of some sort of yellow material that fitted her figure as a glove fits the hand. But more than this one's sight could not distinguish, saving that her hat, that was very wide at the brim, was apparently of straw or chip with one side curled up to a large crimson flower there.

I saw Miss Laura gazing with the fascination of a bird at some gilded and glowing and emerald eyed serpent. Captain Crimp, looking round at his vessel just then, said, 'Them's the parties.'

'Ay, there's her ladyship,' whipped out Finn, biting his lip, however, as though ashamed of the exclamation, with a dodge of his head to right and left as he levelled a look at the couple under the sharp of his hand.

'Finn,' cried Wilfrid with a face as crimson as though he had exposed it to the sun all day, and with a note in his utterance as if his teeth were setting spite of him whilst he spoke, 'get a boat lowered and brought to the gangway. You, myself, Miss Jennings, and my cousin will go aboard that barque at once. Captain Crimp will attend us in his own boat.' He turned swiftly upon the master of the barque and exclaimed imperiously, with wrath surging into his words till it rendered the key of them almost shrill, 'I count upon your assistance. You must order those people off your vessel. Yonder lady is my wife, and the man alongside of her I must have—

here!' stamping his foot and pointing vehemently to the deck, 'that I may punish him. Do you understand me?'

'Why, of course I do,' answered Captain Crimp, manifestly awed by the wild look my cousin fastened upon him, by his manner, full of haughtiness and passion, and his tone of fierce command. 'What I says is, do what ye like, only let me be out of the smother. My crew's troublesome enough. Don't want to get in no mess through castaway folks.'

Finn was yelling orders along the deck for a boat's crew to lay aft.

On a sudden the yacht was hailed by the man whom I had noticed standing near Colonel Hope-Kennedy. 'Schooner ahoy!'

Jacob Crimp went to the rail. 'Hallo!' he bawled.

'Will yer tell my capt'n, please,' shouted the fellow from the barque's quarterdeck, 'that the lady and gent desire him to come aboard, as they don't want nothen to do with your schooner? They prefer to keep where they are, and request that no more time may be lost.'

'Ha!' cried Wilfrid, looking round at me with an iron grin; then he half screamed to the men who were running aft, 'Bear a hand with the boat, my lads, bear a hand with the boat!

We've found what we've been hunting in yonder craft, and by God, men, we'll have that couple out of it or sink the vessel they stand on!'

Jack is almost certain to cheer to a speech of this kind; the sailors burst out into a loud hurrah as they sprang to the falls. Captain Crimp walked to his brother's side, and putting his hand to his mouth cried to the mate of his vessel, for such the fellow undoubtedly was, 'Mr. Lobb.'

'Hillo, sir.'

'My compliments to the lady and gent, and we're *all* a-coming aboard. I don't want no trouble, tell 'em, and I don't mean to have none.'

Scarce was the sense of this remark gatherable when Lady Monson walked to the companion and vanished below, leaving the Colonel standing erect as a sentry at the rail.

'She's gone to her cabin, and will lock herself in probably. What'll be to do then?' said I to Miss Laura.

She wrung her hands, but made no answer.

Meanwhile in hot haste the sailors had cast adrift the gripes of the boat and lowered her. She was a roomy fabric, pulling six oars, and capable of comfortably stowing eighteen or twenty people.

'Mr. Crimp,' said Wilfrid, 'get tackles aloft

ready for swaying out of the hold the eighteen-pounder that lies there. D'ye understand?'

'Ay, it shall be done,' answered Crimp, coming away from his brother, with whom he had been exchanging some muttering sentences.

'An eighteen-pounder!' cried Captain Crimp, whipping round.

'Have everything in readiness,' cried Wilfrid, making a move towards the gangway, 'to get the gun mounted, with ball and cartridge for loading. See to it now, or look to yourself, Crimp. Come!' he cried.

He seized Miss Laura by the hand; Finn and I followed, Captain Crimp rolling astern of us. We descended the side and entered the boat, and then shoved off, waiting when we were within a length or two of the yacht's side for Captain Crimp to drop into his own boat.

'Skipper,' sung out Finn to him, 'hail your barque, will'ee, and tell 'em to get a ladder or steps over.'

This was done; the sailors of the barque, along with the three or four yachtsmen who had been picked up out of the 'Shark's' boat, scenting plenty of excitement in the air, tumbled about with alacrity. They saw more sport than they could have got out of an evening at a theatre, and I question if a man of them could have been got to handle a brace until this wild ocean drama had been played through. Meanwhile the Colonel stood rigid at the rail looking on.

'What is to be done, Mr. Monson,' whispered Miss Laura to me, 'if Henrietta has locked herself up in her cabin and refuses to come out?'

'Let us hope that her door has no lock,' said I. 'There are easy ways, however, of coaxing a bolt.'

'Give way, lads!' cried Finn. The six blades cut the water sharp as knives, and a few strokes carried us alongside the barque. We held a grim silence, saving that as the bow oar picked up his boat-hook he expectorated violently to the evil smell that seemed to come floating off the vessel's side as she rolled towards us, driving the air our way. Evil it was, as you may suppose of a cargo of guano mixed up with the rotting carcases of sea-fowl under the blaze of the sun whose roasting eye of fire was fast crawling to its meridian. The faint breeze was dying, and the heat alongside the barque was scarce sufferable with the tingling of the luminary's light like fiery needles darting into one's eyes and skin off the smooth surface that flashed with a dazzle of new tin. The Colonel had left the rail and had seated himself upon a little skylight, his arms folded.

The first to climb the side was Wilfrid; Finn and I followed, supporting Miss Laura between us; then came Captain Crimp The vessel was an old craft, her decks somewhat grimy, with a worm-eaten look; the smell of the cargo coupled with the heat was hardly supportable; the crew, half naked, unwashed, and many of them wild with hair, stood sweltering in a cluster near the fore-hatch staring at us, grinning and nudging one another. But the men who had belonged to the 'Shark' were already leaning over the side calling to our men to hook their boat more forward that they might have a yarn.

Wilfrid, who was a little in advance of us, walked steadily up to Colonel Hope-Kennedy, who rose as my cousin approached him, letting fall his arms from their folded posture. Handsome he was not, at least to my taste, but he was what would be called a fine man—exceedingly so; six feet one or more in stature, with a body and limbs perfectly proportioned to his height; small dark eyes heavily thatched, coal-black whiskers and moustache, ivory-white teeth, and an expression of intelligence in his face as his air was one of distinction. He had a very care-worn look, was pale, haggard almost; dark hollows under the eyes, brought about, as I might readily suppose, by exposure and privation in an open boat. I could witness no agitation in him whatever; his nerves seemed of steel, and he confronted Wilfrid's approach haughtily erect, merely swaying to the heel of the deck, passionless and as unmoved in his aspect as any figure of wax.

Wilfrid walked right up to him and said composedly whilst he pointed to the gangway, 'You will be good enough to enter my boat that my crew may convey you at once to the yacht.'

'I shall do nothing of the kind, sir,' answered the Colonel quietly, but in a tone distinctly audible to us who had come to a halt some paces away. 'Captain Crimp.'

'Sir?' responded the master of the barque, with an uneasy shuffling step or two towards the couple.

'You are the commander of this vessel. It is in your power to order your deck to be cleared of these visitors. I am your passenger, and look to you for protection. I decline to exchange this vessel for that yacht, and request, therefore, that you will proceed on your voyage.' He spoke with a fine air of dignity, the effect of which was improved, I thought, by his giving himself slightly the manner of an injured man.

'Sir, I want no trouble,' answered Captain Crimp. 'I onderstand that the lady you're with is this gentleman's wife. Every man's got a right to his own. The gentleman means to take the lady back with him to his yacht, and I don't think that there's any one aboard this wessel as'll stop him.'

'I mean to take my wife,' exclaimed Wilfrid, still preserving what in him was an amazing composure of voice and manner, 'and I mean to take you too. Colonel Hope-Kennedy, you are a bloody rascal! You shall fight me—but not here. You shall fight me—yonder;' he pointed to the 'Bride.' '*This* you *must* repay.' He struck him hard upon the face with the back of his hand.

The cheek that had received the blow turned scarlet, the other was of a ghastly pallor. He looked at Wilfrid for a moment with such a fire in his eye, such a hellish expression of wrath in his face, that I involuntarily sprang forward to the help of my cousin, resolved that there should be no vulgar, degraded exhibition of fisticuffs and wrestling between the men.

But I was misled by the Colonel's looks. He folded his arms, and said—exhibiting in his utterance a marvellous control over his temper—'That blow was needless. I will fight you here or on your own vessel, as you please. But if I fight you yonder the condition must be'—he was now looking at me and addressing me—'that I am afterwards at liberty to return to this vessel.'

Wilfrid eyed him with a savage smile. I approached the man, raising my hat. He instantly returned the salute.

'Sir,' I said, 'I am Sir Wilfrid Monson's cousin, and agree to the condition you name. To save any further exhibition of temper before those men there, may I entreat you to at once step into the yacht's boat?'

His eye wandered about the deck for a moment or two; he then said, 'I am without a second. That need not signify. But I must be satisfied that the duel in other respects will be in accordance with the practice of such things ashore.'

'Oh! certainly,' I answered.

'What are to be the weapons?' he inquired.

'Pistols,' I replied.

'I have no pistols. I have lost all by the foundering of my yacht.'

'We have pistols,' said I.

He bowed, then his eye roamed over the deck again, and he exclaimed, with the air of a man thinking aloud, 'I am without a second,' adding decisively, 'I am perfectly willing to give Sir Wilfrid Monson satisfaction, but I submit, sir, that it would be more convenient to wait until he and I have arrived home——'

'No!' thundered my cousin. 'I do not mean that you shall arrive home.'

The Colonel glanced at him with a sneer.

'Will you be so good as to step into the boat, sir?' said I.

He hung in the wind with a look at the little companion hatch. 'The lady, I presume,' he said, addressing me, 'is to be left——'

'Do not mention her name!' said Wilfrid in a trembling voice, approaching him by a stride with a countenance dark with the menace of mad blood.

The Colonel fell away from him with a swiftly passing convulsion of countenance such as might have been wrought by a sudden spasm of the heart.

'This way, sir,' said Finn, moving in a bustling fashion towards the gangway.

I confess I drew a breath of relief when the Colonel, without a word, and with a mechanical step, followed him. There was, indeed, no other course that he could adopt. Captain Crimp had retreated doggedly to the gangway abreast of the one we had entered by, and lay over the rail in a wooden way, with resolution to give himself no concern in this business strong in his posture. The Colonel saw, therefore, that it was useless to hope for his interference. In a few moments he had descended the side, and was being pulled aboard the 'Bride,' with Finn standing up in the stern-sheets and singing out to us that he would return for the rest of the party shortly.

I now missed Miss Laura, and was looking around the deck for her when she suddenly came up out of the cabin. I was standing close to the hatch at the moment, which was the reason, perhaps, of her addressing me instead of Wilfrid, who was at the skylight gazing at the withdrawing boat with an absent face.

'Mr. Monson,' she exclaimed, 'my sister will not answer me. I do not know where she is.'

'Have you tried all the berths?'

'I have knocked at every door and called to her. I did not like to turn the handles.'

I thought to myself, suppose her ladyship has committed suicide!—lying dead below with a knife in her heart! Truly a pleasant ending of our chase, with a chance on top of it of the Colonel driving a bullet through my cousin's brains! The girl's gaze was fastened on me; her pallor was grievous, her face full of shame, grief, consternation; her very beauty had a sort of passing withered look like a rose in the hot atmosphere of a room.

'Wilfrid!' I exclaimed.

He brought his eyes away from the boat with a start and approached us. 'Miss Jennings has been overhauling the cabin below,' said I, 'and cannot get your wife to answer her.'

'Have you seen her, Laura?' he cried in a half-breathless way, stooping his face to hers, with his near-sighted eyes moistening till I looked to see a tear fall.

'No,' she answered. 'She has shut herself up in her cabin. I have knocked at every berth and called to her, but she will not answer me.'

His face changed. He shouted to Captain Crimp, who was leaning with his back against the starboard rail near the gangway, watching us out of the corner of his eyes and waiting for us to take the next step. He came to us.

'Kindly show us,' said Wilfrid, 'the cabin which the lady occupies.'

'This way,' he answered, and forthwith trundled down the companion steps, we at his heels. We found ourselves in what Captain Crimp would doubtless have called a state cabin, a gloomy dirty interior with a board-like rude table that travelled upon stanchions so that it could be thrust up out of the road when room was wanted, whilst on either hand of it was a row of coarse lockers, the covers of which were liberally scored with the marks of knives that had been used for cutting up cake-tobacco. The upper deck was very low pitched, and, as if the heat and the disgusting smell of the cargo did not suffice, there swung from a blackened beam a lighted globular lamp the flame of which burnt into a coil of thick black smoke that filled the atmosphere with a flavour of hot fat. Yet apparently, to judge by the number of berths this rank and grimy old barque was fitted with, she had served as a passenger vessel in her heyday. There were doors conducting to little cabins forward of the living room, and there were four berths abaft contrived much as the 'Bride's' were, that is to say, rendered accessible by a slender alley-way or corridor.

'The lady's cabin,' said Captain Crimp, pointing, 'is the starn one to port, the airiest of 'em all. It was chosen because it was furdest off from this here smell,' and he snuffled as he spoke.

Wilfrid, followed by Miss Laura, at once walked to the indicated cabin. I remained standing by the table with Crimp, watching my cousin. He tried the handle of the door, found the key turned or a bolt shot, shook it a little, then, after a pause, knocked lightly.

'Henrietta,' he exclaimed. 'It is I—your husband. You know my voice. I want you.'

There was no answer. He knocked again,

then Miss Laura exclaimed: 'Henrietta, open the door. Wilfrid is here—I am here, I, Laura your sister. We have come to take you home to the little one that you left behind you. Oh, Henrietta, dear, for my sake—for your child's sake, for our father's sake—' her voice faltered and she broke down, sobbing piteously.

'I hope to heaven the woman has not killed herself,' I exclaimed to Captain Crimp. 'But it is for you to act now. Step aft with me. You don't want to keep her on board, I suppose?'

'Not I,' he answered.

'Threaten then to break open the door. If that don't avail, send at once for your carpenter, for you may then take it that her silence means she lies dead.'

He walked aft and beat with a fist as hard as the stock of a musket, raising a small thunder. 'Sorry to interfere, lady,' he exclaimed, talking at the door with his nose within an inch of it; 'this here's no job for the likes of me to be messing about with.' A dead pause. 'There's folks who are a-waiting for you to come out.' Here he grasped the handle of the door and boisterously shook it. 'And as there's no call now for you to remain, and as loitering in this here heat with the hatches flush with gewhany isn't to none of our liking, I must beg, mum,' he shouted, 'that you'll slip the bolt inside and open the door.'

Another dead pause. Miss Jennings looked aghast, and indeed the stillness within the cabin now caused me to forebode the worst. It was clear, however, that no fear of the sort had visited Wilfrid. He gazed at the door with a kind of terrier-like expression in his fixed eyes.

Captain Crimp once more beat heavily and again wrestled with the handle, trying the door at the same time with his shoulder. 'Well, mum,' he bawled, 'you will do as you like, I suppose, and so must I. I'm not partial to knocking my ship about, but by thunder! lady, if this here door ain't opened at once I'll send for the carpenter to force it.' Another pause. He added in his hoarsest voice, addressing us generally, 'Do she know that the gent that's been keeping her company has gone aboard the yacht?'

'She'll know it now,' I answered, 'if she has ears to hear with.'

I noticed Wilfrid violently start on my saying this.

'Gentlemen,' said Captain Crimp, 'I'll go and fetch the carpenter,' and he had taken a stride when the bolt within was shot, the handle turned and the door opened.

Had we come fresh from the splendour of the

morning on deck we must have had great difficulty in distinguishing objects in the gloom of the little, hot, evil-smelling interior that had been suddenly revealed to us; but the twilight of the narrow passage in which we stood had accustomed our sight to the dim atmosphere. Lady Monson stood before us in the middle of the cabin reared to her fullest stature, her hands clasped in front of her in a posture of passionate resolution. I must confess that she had the noblest figure of any woman I had ever seen, and no queen of tragedy could have surpassed the unconsciously heroic attitude of scorn, indignation, hate, unsoftened by the least air of remorse or shame, that she had assumed.

'Captain Crimp,' she cried in a clear, rich, contralto voice that thrilled through and through one with what I must call the intensity of the emotions it conveyed, 'how *dare* you threaten me with breaking open my door? I am your passenger—you will be paid for the services you have rendered. I demand your protection. Who are these people? Order them to leave your ship, sir.'

She spoke with her eyes glowing and rivetted upon Captain Crimp's awkward, agitated countenance, never so much as glancing at her husband, at her sister, or at me.

'Well, mum,' answered Captain Crimp, passing the back of his hand over his streaming forehead, 'all that I know is this: here's a gentleman as says you're his wife; his yacht lies within heasy reach; he wants you aboard, and if so be that you *are* his wife, which nobody yet has denied, then you're bound to go along with him, and I may as well tell'ee that my dooty as a man lies in seeing that ye *do* go.' And here the old chap very spunkily bestowed several emphatic nods upon her.

'Henrietta,' cried Miss Laura, 'have you nothing to say to me or to Wilfrid?'

'Go!' she shrieked, with a sharp stamp of her foot and a wild, warding off gesture of her arms. 'What right have you to follow me? I am my own mistress. Leave me. The mere sight of you will drive me as mad as *he* is!' pointing impetuously to Wilfrid but without looking at him.

The poor little darling shrunk like a wounded bird, literally cowering behind me, dismayed and terrified, not indeed by the woman's words, but by the passion in them, the air with which she delivered them, the wrath in her face and the fire in her eyes that would have made you think they reflected a sunset. I looked at Wilfrid. Had she exhibited the least grief, the least shame, any the feeblest hint, in short, of womanly weakness, I believe he would have fallen upon his knees to her. I had observed an expression almost of adoration enter into and soften his lineaments to an aspect that I do not exaggerate in calling beautiful through the exquisite pathos of the tenderness that had informed it on her throwing open the door and revealing herself to us; but that look was gone. Her scornful reference to his madness had replaced it by an ugly shadow, a scowl of malignant temper. He stepped over the coaming of the doorway, and extended his hand as if to grasp her.

'Come!' he exclaimed, breathing dangerously fast. 'I want you. This is merely wasting time. Come you *must*! Do you understand? Come!' he repeated, still keeping his arm outstretched.

She recoiled from him as though a cartridge had exploded at her feet and pressed her back against the side of a bunk, the edge of which she gripped with her hands.

'Leave me!' she said, looking at him now. 'I hate you. You cannot control me. I abhor the very memory of you. Madman and wretch! why have you followed me?'

Captain Crimp, who had been shuffling restlessly near me, now whipped in, hoarse, angry and determined; 'See here, mum; all this calling of names isn't going to sarve anybody's purpose. I see how the land lies now. The gentleman has a right to his own, and it's proper ye should know that 'tain't my intention to keep ye. Let there be no more noise aboard this wessel, I beg; otherwise you'll be having my crew shoving down into the cabin to know what's happening. Give her your arm, sir,' he cried, addressing me, 'and lead her to the gangway. Your boat 'll be returned by this time.'

My arm, thought I! Egad, I'd liefer snug the paw of a tigress under my elbow!

'Wilfrid,' I exclaimed, 'let me exhort you to go on deck and take Miss Jennings with you. I am sure Lady Monson will listen to my representations. It is due to her to remember that we are four and that she stands alone, and that the suddenness, the unexpectedness of this visit, scarcely gives her a chance fully to realise what has come about, and to form an intelligent decision.'

She uttered a short hysterical laugh, without a smile, whilst her face glimmered white with rage in the gloom of the cabin. 'My decision is quite intelligent enough to satisfy me,' she said, in a voice so irritatingly scornful that it is out of my power to furnish the least idea of it, whilst she looked at me as though she would strike me dead with her eyes; 'I mean to remain here.'

'No, mum, no,' growled Captain Crimp.

'You know, I presume, Lady Monson,' said I, 'that Colonel Hope-Kennedy has gone on board the "Bride"?'

'I do not care,' she answered; 'Captain Crimp, I insist upon your requesting these people to leave me.'

'Come!' cried Wilfrid furiously, and he grasped her by the arm.

She released herself with a shriek and struck him hard on the face; a painful and disgusting scene was threatened; Miss Jennings was crying bitterly; I dreaded the madman in Wilfrid, and sprang between them as he grasped his wife's arm again.

'For God's sake, Wilfrid——' I began, but was silenced by her shrieks. She sent up scream after scream, wrestling with her husband, whose grip of steel I was powerless to relax and who, with a purple face and a devilish grin of insanity upon his lips, was dragging her towards the door. On a sudden she seemed to suffocate, she beat the air wildly with her arm that was free, then clapped her hand to her heart, swayed a little, and fell to the deck. I was just in time to save her head from striking the hard plank, and there she lay in a dead faint.

## CHAPTER XXIV.

### THE DUEL

'This is our chance,' exclaimed Captain Crimp; 'she'll go quietly now. She might have done it afore, though. Let's bear a hand, or she'll be reviving.'

'Wilfrid, see if our boat's alongside, will you?' I cried, anxious to get him out of the way and to correct as far as possible the unmistakable mood of madness that had come upon him with Lady Monson's insults and blow, by finding him occupation; 'and send Finn to help us, and let the men stand by, ready to receive the lady.'

He cast a look of fury at his wife as she lay motionless on the deck, her head supported on my arm, and sped away in long strides, chattering to himself as he went.

'Is she dead?' cried Miss Jennings, in a voice of terror and her ashen face streaming.

'Bless us, no,' said I, 'a downright faint, and thank goodness for it. Now, captain.'

How between us we managed to carry her on deck, I'm sure I do not know. Captain Crimp had her by the feet, I by the shoulders, and Miss Laura helped to keep the apparently lifeless woman's head to its bearings. She was as limber as though struck by lightning, and the harder to carry for that reason,—a noble figure, as I have said, and deucedly heavy to boot. My part was the hardest, for I had to step backwards and mount the companion ladder, that was almost perpendicular, crab-fashion. The captain and I swayed together, staggering and perspiring, bothered excessively by the ungainly rolling of the barque, both of us nearly dead with heat, and I half suffocated besides by the abominable acid stench from the hold. We were animated, however, into uncommon exertions by the desire to get her over the side before she recovered; and the fear of her awakening and resisting us and shrieking out, and the like, gave us, I reckon, for that particular job the strength of four men. We conveyed her to the gangway, helped by Finn, who received us at the companion hatch, and with infinite pains handed her over the side, still motionless in her swoon, into the boat. A hard task it was; we durst not call out, for fear of reviving her, and the melancholy business was carried through by signs and gestures, topped off with sundry hoarse whispered orders from Finn.

I paused panting, my face burning like fire, whilst Captain Crimp looked to be slowly dissolving, the perspiration literally streaming from his fingers' ends on to the deck as though he were a figure of snow gradually wasting.

'Why couldn't she have fainted away at first?' he muttered to me. 'That's the worst of women. They're always so slow a-making up their minds.'

Now that she was in the boat the trouble was at an end; though she recovered consciousness she could not regain the barque's deck, and there was no power in her screams to hinder the yachtsmen's oars from sweeping her to the 'Bride.' Preserve me! What a picture it all made just then: the wild-haired, wild-eyed, semi-nude figures of the barque's crew overhanging the rail to view Lady Monson as she lay white and corpse-like in the bottom of the boat; the sober, concerned faces of our own men; Wilfrid's savage, crazy look as he waited with his eyes fixed upon his yacht for Miss Laura to be handed down before entering the boat himself; the prostrate form of his wife with her head pillowed on Finn's jacket, her eyes half opened, disclosing the whites only, and imparting the completest imaginable aspect of death to her countenance with its pale lips and marble brow and cheek bleached into downright ghastliness by contrast of the luxuriant black hair that had fallen in tresses from under her hat. The men who had belonged to the 'Shark' stood in a little group near the foremast looking on, but with a commiserating, respectful air. One of them stepped up to us as Miss Laura was in the act of descending the side, and addressing Finn whilst he touched his cap, exclaimed, 'We should be glad, sir, if you'd take us aboard the "Bride." We'll heartily tarn to with the rest; you'll find us all good men.'

'No!' roared Wilfrid, whipping round upon him, 'I want no man that has had anything to do with the "Shark" aboard my vessel.'

The fellow fell back muttering. My cousin turned to Captain Crimp.

'Sir,' he cried, 'I thank you for your friendly offices.' He produced a pocket-book. 'You have acted the part of an honest man, sir. I am obliged to you. I trust that this may satisfy all charges for the maintenance of Lady Monson on board your ship.' He handed him a Bank of England note; Crimp turned the corner down to look at the figure—I believe it was a hundred pounds—and then buried it in his breeches pocket.

'I'm mighty obliged to you, mighty obliged,' he exclaimed. 'It's a deal more'n the job's worth. I'd like to see my way to wishing you happiness'—and he was proceeding, but Wilfrid stopped him by dropping over the side, calling to me to make haste.

'Captain Crimp,' I said hurriedly, 'you will please keep your barque hove-to as she is now for the present. There's to be a duel; you of course know that.' He nodded. 'You also heard the promise made to Colonel Hope-Kennedy, that after the duel he is to be at liberty to return to your vessel.'

'Then I don't think he will, for the guv'nor means to shoot him,' said Captain Crimp, 'and I'll wager what he guv me that he'll do it too; and sarve 'im right. Running away with another man's wife! Ain't there enough single gals in the world to suit the likes of that there colonel? But I'll keep hove-to as you ask.'

All this he mumbled in my ear as I put my foot over the side waiting for the wash of the swell to float the boat up before dropping. We then shoved off.

We had scarcely measured a boat's length, however, from the barque's side when Lady Monson stirred, opened and shut her eyes, drew a long, fluttering breath, then started up, leaning on her elbow staring about her. She gazed at the men, at me, at her husband and sister, with her wits abroad, but intelligence seemed to rush into her eyes like fire when her sight encountered the yacht. I thought to myself what will she do now? Jump overboard? Go into hysterics? Swoon away again? I watched her keenly, though furtively, prepared to arrest any passionate movement in her, for there had come a wilder look in her face than ever I had seen in Wilfrid's. My cousin sat like a figure of stone, his gaze rivetted to his schooner, and Miss Laura glanced at her sister wistfully, but, as one saw, on the alert to avoid meeting her gaze.

I could very well understand now that this fair, gentle, golden-haired girl should have held her tall, dark, imperious, tragic-eyed sister in awe.

I know I felt heartily afraid of her myself as I sat pretending not to notice her, though in an askant way I was taking her in from head to foot, feeling mightily curious to see what sort of a person she was, and I was exceedingly thankful that the yacht lay within a few minutes of us. But happily there was to be no 'scene.' She saw how things stood, and with an air of haughty dignity rose from the bottom of the boat and seated herself in the place I vacated for her, turning her face seawards to conceal it from the men.

Nobody but a woman possessed of her excellent harmonious shape could have risen unaided with the grace, I may say the majesty, of motion she exhibited from the awkward, prostrate posture in which she had lain. The bitter, sarcastic sneer upon her lip paralysed in me the immediate movement of my mind to offer her my hand. She seemed to float upwards to her full height as a stage dancer of easy and exquisite skill rises to her feet from a recumbent attitude. I might well believe that many men would find her face fascinating, though it was not one that I could fall in love with. She was out and away handsomer than her picture represented her, spite of the traces which yet lingered of suffering, privation, and distress of mind, such as shipwreck and even a day's tossing about in an open boat might produce.

Not a syllable was uttered by any one of us as the flashing oars of the rowers swept us to the 'Bride.' The sailors with instinctive good feeling stared to right and left at their dripping and sparkling blades as though absorbed by contemplation of the rise and fall of the sand-white lengths of ash. Finn at the yoke-lines sat with a countenance of wood. We buzzed foaming to the accommodation ladder. I was the first to spring out, and stood waiting to hand Lady Monson on to the steps; but without taking the least notice of me she exclaimed, addressing her sister in a low but distinctly audible voice, 'Take me at once to your cabin,' and so saying she stepped on to the ladder. I helped Miss Laura out of the boat, and then they both passed through the gangway and I saw no more of them. Wilfrid mounted slowly at my heels. I passed my arm through his and walked him aft. He made as if he would resist, then came passively enough, sighing deeply as though his heart had broken.

'Wilfrid,' I said gently, 'a hard and bitter part of the project of your voyage is ended. You have regained your wife—your one desire is fulfilled. Why not, then, abandon the rest of your programme? Yonder barque will be kept hove to until we hail her to say that she may proceed. Colonel Hope-Kennedy does not want to fight you. Let me go to him and arrange that he shall return to that vessel forthwith? I abhor the notion of a duel between you. Your end has been achieved bloodlessly; your baby has such a claim upon your life, that if you will but give a moment's thought to the significance of it, you would not, you dare not, turn a deaf ear to the infant's appeal. Consider again, we are without a surgeon; there is no medical help here for the sufferer, be he you or be he your enemy. This colonel, again, is without a second. Wilfrid, in the name of God, let him go! He may reach England, and will meet you ashore, if you desire it; but between then and now there will be abundance of time for you to consider whether there is any occasion for you to give the scoundrel a chance of completing the injury he has already dealt you by sending a bullet through your heart.'

He listened to me with wonderful patience, his head bowed, his eyes rooted on the deck, his hands clasped in front of him. I was flattering myself that I had produced something of the impression I desired to make, when, lifting his face, he looked slowly round at me, and said quietly, almost softly, 'Charles, I shall not love you less for your advice. You speak out of the fulness of your heart. I thank you, dear cousin, for your kindness. And now do me this favour.' He pulled out his watch and let his eye rest on it for a brief pause, but I doubt if he took note of the hour. 'Go to Colonel Hope-Kennedy and make all necessary arrangements for our meeting as soon as possible. See Captain Finn, and request him to send the sailors below when the appointed time arrives. Come to my cabin and let me know the result. Colonel Hope-Kennedy shall have choice of the pistols in my case, and, seeing that he has no second any more than I have, for your office will simply consist in chalking the distance and in giving the signal, he must load for himself.'

He took my hand in both his, pressed it hard, and then, without a word, walked to the companion and disappeared. Captain Finn, who had been watching us from a distance, waiting till our conversation had ended, now walked up to me.

'Can you tell me his honour's wishes, sir?' he inquired. 'I suppose now that he's fallen in with her ladyship he'll be heading home?'

'Let the yacht lie as she is for the present, Finn,' said I; 'no need to hoist in the boat either. She cannot hurt herself alongside in this smooth water. We may be wanting her shortly to convey Colonel Hope-Kennedy to the barque. Sir Wilfrid means to fight him, and at once. I would give half what I am worth to avert this meeting, but my cousin is resolved, and I must stand by him.'

'Sir,' said Finn, 'he has been cruelly used.'

'When the time comes,' I continued, 'he wishes the men to be sent below. You will see to that.'

'Oh, yes. But I dorn't think the helm should be desarted, sir.'

'Certainly not,' I exclaimed. 'Arrange it thus: Let Mr. Crimp hold the wheel. I must have help at hand, for one of the men may fall badly wounded. Therefore, stay you on deck, Captain Finn, and keep by me within easy hail. Cutbill is also a strong, serviceable fellow in such an emergency as this. Post him at the forehatch to hinder any man from popping his head up to look. I shall thus have two—you and him—to assist me.'

'Right, sir,' he exclaimed, touching his cap.

'Better mark off the ground, or deck rather, at once,' said I; 'fetch me a piece of chalk, Finn.'

He went forward, and in a few moments returned with what I required. A broad awning sheltered the whole of the quarterdeck that lay gleaming white as the flesh of the cocoa-nut in the soft, almost violet-hued shadow. There was just air enough stirring aloft to keep the lighter cloths quiet and to provide against the yacht being slued or revolved by the run of the long, delicate, tropic swell. I said to Finn, after considering a little and anxiously observing the effects of the sunshine gushing through the blue air betwixt the edge of the awning and the bulwark rail, or rising off the sea in a trembling flashing that whitened the air above it, 'I don't think it will matter which side of the quarterdeck we choose. The men must toss for position. But there's a dazzle on the water off the port bow that might bother the eye that faces forward. Better mark the starboard side therefore.'

He gazed thoughtfully around, and said, 'The yacht's position can be altered, if you like, sir.'

I answered, 'No; leave her as she is. She rolls regularly and quietly thus.'

I had never before been concerned in a duel, and in the matter of the strict etiquette of this sort of encounter was entirely at a loss how to act. However, I had always understood that twelve paces were the prescribed distance, so ruling a line athwartships almost abreast of the mainmast, I made twelve steps and then scored another line crosswise, measuring the interval a second time, and finding that it was very fairly twelve of my own paces. The men had come together in a crowd forward, and were staring aft with all their might. They knew perfectly well what was going to take place, and they were not yet sensible that they were not to be admitted to the spectacle. It was to be something of a far more wildly exciting sort than catching a shark, aye, or even may be of seeing a man hung at a ship's yardarm. It put a sort of sickness into me somehow to witness that swarm of whiskered mahogany-cheeked faces, all looking thirstily, expectation shaping every posture, with a kind of swimming of the whole body of them too in the haze of heat into which the yacht's jibboom went twisting in a manner to make the brain dizzy to watch it. One never gets to see how thoroughly animal human nature is at bottom until one has examined the expression of the countenances of a mob, big or little, assembled in expectation of witnessing human suffering.

I stepped below. Colonel Hope-Kennedy sat bareheaded at the cabin table, supporting his head on his right elbow and drumming softly with the fingers of his left hand. I approached him, and giving him a bow, which he returned with an air of great dignity—men are amazingly polite when arranging the terms of some cut-throat job—I said, 'It is my painful duty, sir, to inform you that my cousin desires the meeting between you and him should take place at once.'

'Not a moment need be lost so far as I am concerned,' he answered, gazing at me steadfastly with eyes that looked like porcelain with the singular glaze that seemed to have come suddenly upon them.

'My cousin requests me to state,' I continued, 'that you will consider him as acting without a second equally with yourself. My unhappy office will consist simply in giving the signal to fire. I would to God that my influence had been powerful enough with him to arrest his resolution at this point——'

'It could not have prevailed with me,' he exclaimed. 'The madman's blow was needless. On what part of the yacht do we fight?'

'On the quarterdeck,' I answered.

'Measured by you?'

I bowed.

'As there are no seconds,' he said, 'I presume we load for ourselves?'

'That is Sir Wilfrid Monson's suggestion,' I answered.

'Have you the pistols, sir?'

'I will fetch them.'

I went at once to Wilfrid's berth and knocked and walked in without waiting for him to tell me to enter. He was writing in his diary; he instantly threw down his pen and jumped from his chair.

'Is all ready, Charles?' he asked.

'Your pistols are identical, I believe?' said I.

'Exactly alike,' he answered.

'Then Colonel Hope-Kennedy's choice,' said I, 'cannot furnish him with any advantage over you, by his choosing, I mean, with a soldier's experience the preciser weapon?'

'There is not an atom of difference between

them,' he exclaimed. 'Yonder's the case, Charles. Take it, and let the scoundrel choose for himself.'

He could not have spoken more coolly had he been giving me the most commonplace instructions. I remember wondering whilst I looked at him and listened to him whether he actually realised his own intention; yet I should have known better than this if only for the meaning his face conveyed, and for a note in his voice that made every accent hard and steady. He said, 'When you are ready ring the hand-bell on the table; I will then join you.'

'But you will charge your own pistol,' said I, 'so I must return with the weapon after the Colonel has made his choice.'

'No,' he exclaimed; 'carry the case on deck and load for me.'

'Very well,' said I, wearily and sick at heart, and devoutly wishing that some heavy black squall would come thundering down on the yacht as the precursor of a gale of wind and delay this wretched business, for the present, anyway, I took the pistol-case and returned it to Colonel Hope-Kennedy. He slightly glanced at the fire-arms, and said with a faint smile, 'They are an elegant brace of weapons. Either will do for me.'

'Will you load on deck or here, sir?' said I.

'Here, if you please.'

He extracted one of the pistols, poised it in his hand, toying a moment or two with it, tried the trigger once or twice, then loaded it, fitting the cap to the nipple with fingers in which I could not discern the least tremor. He then returned the pistol to the case. Both of us would know which one he had handled very well, as it lay against the side upon which the lid locked.

'Have you a surgeon on board?' he inquired.

I answered No. He looked a little anxious, and exclaimed, 'No one of any kind qualified to deal with a wound?' Again I answered No. He seemed to wince at this, the only expression of uneasiness I had witnessed in him. Finding he asked no more questions, I said, 'If you are ready, sir, I will summon my cousin.'

'I am ready,' he replied.

On this I rang the little hand-bell that stood upon the table, and in a minute Wilfrid came out. In grim silence we mounted the companion steps, my cousin leading the way, the Colonel next, and I at his heels, with the pistol-case under my arm and a very lively sense of murder in my heart. All was hushed where the ladies were. Whether Miss Laura guessed what was going forward I know not, but I was very thankful that she remained hidden, since, in the face of the Colonel's coolness, it was most important that nothing should imperil Wilfrid's composure. The yacht's decks were deserted save by the figures of the men who it had been arranged were to remain. Forward at the hatch conducting to the forecastle stood the tall, burly figure of Cutbill: close beside the cabin skylight was Finn, pale, agitated, his mouth working in the middle of his face as though he were rehearsing a long speech; Crimp grasped the wheel. Heaven knows how it was that I should have found eyesight for small outside features of such a scene as this at that moment, but I clearly recollect observing that sour old Jacob, with a view, mayhap, of supporting his spirits, had thrust an immense quid into his cheek, the angle whereof stood out like a boil or a formidable bruise against the clear gleam of sky past him up and down which the curtseying of the yacht slided his squab, homely figure, and I also observed that he gnawed upon this junk with an energy that suggested a mind in an advanced stage of distraction.

I said to the Colonel, 'It will be satisfactory to myself, sir, if you will kindly measure the distance I have chalked.'

His eye swiftly ran from line to line, and then giving me a slight bow he said, nonchalantly, 'I am quite satisfied.'

'With regard to the light,' I continued, looking from him to Wilfrid, 'you will decide for yourselves, gentlemen, which end of the vessel you will face.'

'It is immaterial,' said the Colonel, with a slight shrug.

'Then,' said Wilfrid, 'I will have my back to the wheel.'

I could not be sure that he was well advised, for the blue dazzle of sunshine past the awning would throw out his figure into clear relief, as I noticed Crimp's was projected, clean lined as a shadow cast by the moonlight on a white deck.

'It may be as well to toss for position,' I said.

'No,' cried Wilfrid, 'I am content.'

I loaded his pistol and handed the weapons to the men. My heart thumped like a coward's in my breast, but I strove hard to conceal my agitation for Wilfrid's sake. Each took up his respective post, and both held their pistols at level. The Colonel exclaimed, 'Tell your mad relative to feather-edge himself. He is all front. 'Tis too irrational to take advantage of.'

Wilfrid heard him and cried out, 'Let him look to himself. Ready with the signal, Charles.'

I pulled out my pocket-handkerchief, and as I did so old Crimp suddenly let go the wheel and came skimming up to Finn, rumbling out, in a voice half choked with tobacco juice, that the gent's pistol (meaning the Colonel's) was upon him full, and that he wasn't going to be made cold beef of for any man.

'Ready, gentlemen!' I cried, and desirous of emphasising the signal, lest the Colonel's keener sight should witness the fall of the handkerchief before the flutter of it caught Wilfrid's eye, I called out '*Now!*' and the handkerchief fell to the deck.

There was one report only; it was like the sharp crack of a whip. For the instant I did not know which man's pistol had exploded, but the little curl of smoke at Wilfrid's end told me that it was his. I saw the Colonel fling his arms up, and his weapon flashed as he seemed to fire it straight into the air. 'Good God! how generous!' was the thought that swept through me; 'he will not fight.' He continued holding his pistol elevated whilst you could have counted ten, with a slight backward leaning posture and an indescribable look in his face, absolutely as though he were endeavouring to follow the flight of the bullet; his weapon then fell to the deck, he made a clutch with both hands at his heart, with a deep groan sank—his knees yielding, and, with his hands still at his heart, dropped, as a wooden figure might, on his side and lay without motion.

Finn and I rushed up to him. Whilst the skipper freed his neck I grasped his wrist, but found it pulseless. Yet it was difficult to credit that he was dead. His face was as reposeful as that of a sleeper. There was no look whatever of pain in it—nay, such faint distinguishable expression as I remember had the air of a light smile. I opened his coat, and found a small perforation in the shirt under the right arm; the orifice was as cleanly clipped as though made with a pair of scissors. There was no blood.

'Dead, sir!' exclaimed Finn. 'A noble-looking gentleman, too. A pity, a pity! How gents of this kind stand upon their honour! yet they're the people to break up homes.'

'Call Cutbill,' said I, 'and let the body be taken below.'

I rose from my knees and walked aft to Wilfrid, who remained standing at the chalked line, his arm that grasped the pistol hanging by his side. There was a kind of *lifting* look in his face, that with his swelled nostrils and large protruding eyes and a curve of the upper lip, that was made a sarcastic sneer of by the peculiar projection of the under one, indicated a mood of scornful triumph, of exultation subdued by contempt.

'You have killed your man, Wilfrid,' said I.

'I have shot him through the heart,' said he,

talking like one newly aroused from his slumber and still in process of collecting his mind.

'Most probably. You hit him in some vital part, anyway. He dropped dead.'

'He made sure of killing me; I saw it in his cold, deliberate way of covering me.' He laughed harshly and mirthlessly. 'He'll trouble no other man's peace. I've merely liberated the spirit of a devil that is now winging its way on black, bat-like wings back to that hell it came from. There will be disappointment amongst the fiends. That fellow there,' nodding at the body over which Cutbill and Finn were bending, 'was good at least for another twenty years of scoundrelism. What are they going to do with him?'

'Carry him below.'

'Finn!' he called.

'Sir!' answered the skipper, looking up from the body, whose arms he grasped.

'Hide it in some forward cabin, and if stone-dead, as Mr. Monson declares, get it stitched up. I'll tell you when to bury him.'

'Ay, ay, sir,' answered Finn promptly, but looking shocked nevertheless.

My cousin handed me his pistol. As he did so his manner changed; a broken-hearted look—I do not know how else to describe the expression—entered his face. He drew a long, deep breath, like to the sigh of a sufferer from some exquisite throe, and said in a low voice, trembling with the tears which pressed close behind, 'His death does not return to me what he has taken from me. With him go my honour, my peace of mind, the love that was my wife's—all gone—all gone!' he muttered. 'My God!' he almost shrieked, 'how blank has the world become, now that he lies there.'

'Be advised by me, Wilfrid,' said I; 'withdraw to your cabin and rest. This has been a terrible morning—enough to last out a lifetime has been crowded into it. You met him bravely, fairly, honourably. He has paid the penalty of his infamy, and though Heaven knows I would have gone to any lengths to avert this meeting, yet, since it has happened, I thank God your life is preserved and that you have come out of it unharmed.'

His eyes moistened and he took my hand; but just then Cutbill and Finn came staggering towards the companion hatch, bearing the body between them, on which he walked hastily to the rail and stood peering over into the water, supporting his temples in his hands.

Jacob Crimp had resumed his hold of the wheel. I went up to him. 'I'll keep the helm steady,' said I, 'whilst you wipe out those chalk marks on the deck. Meanwhile pick up that pistol yonder and bring me the case off the sky-light.'

Whilst he did this we were hailed from the barque. She lay close to us, with her sailors in a crowd about the fore-rigging, where they had been standing attentive spectators of the duel. 'Beg pardon!' bawled Captain Crimp, erect on the rail and steadying himself by a backstay, 'but I should be glad to know if the gent's coming aboard?'

I shouted back, 'No. You need not wait for him.'

The man tossed his arm with a gesture very significant of a growling 'Well, well!' and then with a flourish of his hat he cried, 'A lucky run home to 'ee, gentlemen all!' dismounted, and fell to singing out orders. His wild-looking crew ran about, the maintopsail-yard slowly swang round, and presently the deeply-laden, malodorous craft, rolling clumsily upon a swell to whose light summer heavings our yacht was curtseying with fairy grace, was heading round to her course, blurring the water at her bows to the blowing of the mild breeze that had scarcely power enough to lift her foresail.

Finn and Cutbill arrived on deck, and Wilfrid on seing them went below.

'Better turn the hands up, I suppose, now,

sir?' said Finn to me. 'There'll be nothen more, your honour, that'll be onfit for them to see.'

'By all means, Captain Finn; and then get the boat hoisted and a course shaped for home, for our quest is over, and we have made southing enough, Heaven knows!'

Cutbill went forward. There is a magic in the mere sound of *homeward bound* that would put a jocund nimbleness into the proportions of a marine Falstaff. Cutbill tried to walk and look as though he were sensible that death lay under his feet and that the shadow of a dreadful event hung dark upon the yacht, but scarce was he abreast of the galley when his spirits proved too much for him, and he measured the rest of the deck in several gleesome, floundering jumps, pounding the scuttle with a capstan bar that he snatched up, and roaring out, 'All hands trim sail for home!' The men came tumbling up as though the yacht's forecastle were vomiting sailors, and in a breath the lustrous decks of the 'Bride' were full of life, colour, and movement.

A man came to the wheel. I lingered a minute or two to exchange a few words with Finn.

'You are sure the Colonel is dead?'

'Ay, sir; he'll be no deader a thousand years hence.'

'A bloody morning's work, Finn! I feel

heart-sick, as though I had shared in the assassination of a man. But since it was bound to end in one or the other's death, 'tis best as it is. Have you any particulars of the foundering of the "Shark?"'

'The yarn her people—I mean the surwivors aboard the barque—spun our men whilst they lay alongside was that they met with a gale of wind, that, after blowing with hurricane fury for two days and two nights, ended in dismasting 'em. The fall of the mainmast ripped the plank out of the deck as clean as though shipwrights had been at work there. Then the pounding of the wreckage alongside started a butt, and she took in water faster than they could pump it out. There were boats enough for all hands and to spare, and they had just time to get away when the "Shark" foundered. 'Twas blowing hard then and a high sea running, and before it came on dark the boats had lost sight of one another. The Colonel and her ladyship were together, along with five sailors, one of whom fell overboard on the second day and was drownded. They was three days and four nights washing about afore the "'Liza Robbins" fell in with them. That's all I got to hear, sir; but I suppose it's the true yarn right enough.'

'I dare say they encountered much such weather as we met with,' said I; 'the same straight-lined storm thundering up from the south, for all one knows. Well, now, Finn, drive us home as fast as ever you can. Bowl her along—we've all had enough of it. In what berth have you placed the body?'

'In the one that was occupied by his honour's walet, sir.'

I gave him a nod, and, with the pistol-case under my arm, descended the steps and went to my cabin.

## CHAPTER XXV.

### THE COLONEL'S FUNERAL.

On entering my berth I threw myself into my bunk and sat in it in such a despondent condition of mind as I had never before been sensible of. This, to be sure, signified no more than reaction following the wild excitement I had been under all the morning. But, let the cause be what it might, whilst the fit was on me I felt abjectly miserable and a complete wretch. It then occurred to me that hunger might have something to do with my mood, seeing that no food had crossed my lips since dinner time on the preceding day.

It was about two o'clock in the afternoon. I entered the cabin and found a cold lunch upon the table, not a dish of which had been touched, proving that there were others besides myself who were fasting. I was without appetite, but I sat down resolutely, and, calling to the steward—who seemed thankful to have an order to attend to—to bring me a bottle of Burgundy, I fell to, and presently found myself tolerably hearty ; the fountain of my spirits unsealed afresh, and beginning leisurely to bubble into the channel that had run dry. There is no better specific in the world for a fit of the blues than a bottle of Burgundy. No other wine has its art of tender blandishments. It does not swiftly exhilarate, but courts the brain into a pleasing serenity by a process of coaxing at once elegant and convincing.

Whilst I sat fondling my glass, leaning back in my chair with my eyes fixed upon the delicate, graceful paintings on the cabin ceiling, and my mind revolving, but no longer blackly and weepingly, the grim incidents which had crowded the morning, I heard my name pronounced close at my ear, and, whipping round, found Miss Laura at my elbow.

'I have been most anxious to see you,' she exclaimed. 'What is the news?'

'Have not you heard?' I inquired.

'I have heard nothing but two pistol shots. I have seen nobody of whom I could ask a question.'

'Wilfrid has shot Colonel Hope-Kennedy through the heart,' said I, 'as he declared he would, and the body lies yonder;' and I pointed to the recess that Muffin had formerly occupied.

'Colonel Hope-Kennedy killed!' she exclaimed, in a low, breathless, terrified voice; and she sank into a chair beside me, and leant her face on her hand speechless, and her eyes fixed upon the table.

'Better that he should have been shot than Wilfrid,' said I. 'But he is dead; of him then let us speak nothing since we cannot speak good. I have just succeeded in fighting myself out of a hideous mood of melancholy with the help of yonder bottle. Now you must let me prescribe for you. You have eaten nothing since dinner yesterday. I therefore advise a glass of champagne and a slice of the breast of cold fowl;' and that she might not say no, I put on an air of bustle, called to the steward to immediately open a pint bottle of champagne, helped her to a little piece of the fowl, and, finding her still reluctant, gently insinuated a knife and fork into her hands. 'We are homeward bound,' said I: 'see! the sun has slipped t'other side of the yacht. Our bowsprit points directly for dear old Southampton Water. So,' said I, filling a glass of champagne and handing it to her, 'you must absolutely drink to our prosperous voyage, not only to the ship that goes, but to the wind that blows, whilst,' said I, helping myself to another small dose of Burgundy, 'I'll drink the lass that loves a sailor.'

She could not forbear a slight smile, drank and then ate a little, and presently I saw how much good it did her by the manner in which she plucked up her heart. I asked her where Lady Monson was.

'In my cabin,' she answered; 'she will not speak to me; she asks my maid for what she requires; she will not even look at me.'

'It is all too fresh yet,' said I. 'A little patience, Miss Jennings. The woman in her will break through anon: there will be tears, kisses, contrition. Who knows?'

She shook her head. Just then I caught sight of the maid, and beckoned to her, exclaiming to Miss Laura, 'Your sister must not be allowed to starve. I fear she will have known what hunger is aboard Captain Crimp's odious old barque, where the choicest table delicacy probably was rancid salt pork. Here,' said I to the maid, 'get me a tray. Steward, open another bottle of champagne. You will smile at the cook-like view I take of human misery, Miss Jennings,' said I; 'but let me tell you that a good deal of the complexion the mind wears is shed upon it by the body.'

I filled the tray the maid brought, and bade

her carry it to her ladyship, and to let her suppose it was prepared by the steward. I then thought of Wilfrid, and told Miss Laura that I would visit him. 'But you will stop here till I return,' said I. 'I want you to cheer me up.'

I went to my cousin's cabin and knocked very softly. The berth occupied by Lady Monson was immediately opposite, and the mere notion of her being so near made me move with a certain stealth, though I could not have explained why I did so. There was no response, so, after knocking a second time very lightly and obtaining no reply, I entered. Wilfrid lay in his bunk. The porthole was wide open, and a pleasant draught of air breezed into the cabin. He lay in his shirt, the collar of which was wide open, and a pair of silk drawers, flat on his back, his arms crossed upon his breast, like the figure of a knight on a tomb, and his eyes closed. I was startled at first sight of him, but quickly perceived that his breast rose and fell regularly, and that, in short, he was in a sound sleep. Quite restful his slumber was not, for whilst I stood regarding him he made one or two wry faces, frowned, smiled, muttered, but without any nervous starts or discomposure of his placid posture. I was seized with a fit of wonder, and looked about me for some signs of an opiate or for any hint of liquor that should account for this swift and easy repose, but there was nothing of the sort to be seen. He had fallen asleep as a tired child might, or as one who, having accomplished some great object through stress of bitter toil and distracting vigil, lightly pillows his head with a thanksgiving that he has seen the end. I returned to Miss Jennings marvelling much, and she was equally astonished.

'Conceive, Mr. Monson,' she exclaimed, 'that the whole may have passed out of his memory!'

'I wish I could believe it,' said I. 'No, he has just lain down as a boy might who is tired out and dropped asleep. A man is to be envied for being wrong-headed sometimes. If *I* had shot the Colonel—— but we agreed not to speak of him. Miss Jennings, you are better already. When you arrived just now you were white, your eyes were full of worry and care, you looked as if you would never smile again. Now the old sparkle is in your gaze, and *now* you smile once more, and your complexion has gathered afresh that golden delicacy which I must take the liberty of vowing as a friend I admire as a most surprising perfection in you.'

'Oh, Mr. Monson,' she exclaimed softly, with one of those little pouts I was now used to and glad to observe in her again, whilst something of colour came into her cheeks, 'this is no time for compliments.'

Nevertheless she did not seem ill pleased, spite of her looking downwards with a gravity that was above demureness. At that moment Cutbill and Crimp came down the companion ladder, pulling off their caps as they entered. The big sailor had a roll of what resembled sail-cloth under his arm. They passed forward and disappeared in the cabin that had been occupied by Muffin. Miss Laura noticed them, but made no remark. It was impossible that she should suspect their mission. But the sight of them darkened the brighter mood that had come to me out of the companionship of the girl, and I fell grave on a sudden.

'Will you share your cabin with your sister?' I asked.

'No; she cannot bear my presence. My maid will prepare for me the berth adjoining my old one. She must be humoured. Who can express the agonies her pride is costing her?'

'I fear Wilfrid sleeps rather too close to her ladyship,' said I. 'There's a cabin next mine. I should like to see him in it. Figure his taking it into his head in an ungovernable fit of temper to walk in upon his wife——'

'If such an impulse as that visited him,' she answered, 'it would be all the same even if he should sleep amongst the crew forward. Do not anticipate trouble, Mr. Monson. The realities are fearful enough.'

I smiled at her beseeching look. 'Lucky for your sister,' said I, 'that you are on board. She arrives without a stitch saving what she stands up in, and here she finds your wardrobe, the two-score conveniences of the lady's toilet table and a maid on top of it all, with pins and needles and scissors, bodkins and tape—bless me! what a paradise after the "'Liza Robbins."' And then I told her how the 'Shark' was lost, giving her the yarn as I had it from Finn. 'Anyway,' said I, 'Lady Monson is rescued. Your desire is fulfilled.'

'But I did not wish her—I did not want Colonel Hope-Kennedy killed,' she exclaimed with a shudder.

'Yet you could have shot him,' said I; 'do you remember our chat that night off the Isle of Wight?'

'Yes, perfectly well,' she answered. 'But now that he is dead—oh, it is too terrible to think of,' she added with a sob in her voice.

'It must always be so with generous natures,' I exclaimed. 'What is abhorrent to them in life, death converts into a pathetic appeal. Best perhaps to leave old Time to revenge one's wrongs. And now that her ladyship is on board, what is Wilfrid going to do with her?'

'She is never likely to leave her cabin,' she replied.

'When the "Bride" arrives home then?'

'I cannot tell.'

'Had Wilfrid's misfortune been mine this is the consideration that would have stared me in the face from the very start and hindered me from taking any step that did not conduct me straight to the Divorce Court.'

Here her maid arrived and whispered to her, on which, giving me a pretty little sad smile, she rose and went to her cabin. I mounted to the deck and found the wide ocean shivering and flashing under a pleasant breeze of wind whose hot buzzing as it hummed like the vast insect life of a tropic island through the rigging and into the canvas was cooled to the ear by the pleasant noise of running waters on either hand. My first look was for the ''Liza Robbins,' and I was not a little surprised to find her far away down upon our lee quarter, a mere dash of light of a moonlike hue. Finn was pacing the quarterdeck solemnly with a Sunday air upon him. On seeing me he approached with a shipshape salute and exclaimed:

'I suppose there is no doubt, sir, his honour designs that we should be now steering for home?'

'For what other part of the world, captain?'

'Well, sir, at sea one wants instructions. Maybe Sir Wilfrid *knows* that we're going home?'

'He lies sleeping as soundly and peacefully, Finn, as a little boy in his cabin, and knows nothing.'

'Lor' bless me!' cried Finn.

'But you may take me as representing him,' said I, 'and I'll be accountable for all misdirections. About the funeral now. I observed Cutbill and Crimp pass through the cabin. They've gone to stitch the body up.'

'Yes, sir. His honour told me to get it done at once. 'Sides, 'tain't a part of the ocean in which ye can keep the like of them things long.'

'When do you mean to bury him?'

'Well, I thought to-night, sir, in the first watch. Better make a quiet job of it, I allow, for fear of——' and screwing up his face into a peculiar look, he pointed significantly to the deck with clear reference to Lady Monson.

'You are right, Finn. We have had "scenes" enough, as scrimmages are called by women.'

'Will your honour read the orfice?'

'D'ye mean the burial service? It will be hard to see print by lantern light.'

'I've got it, sir, in a book with the letters as big as my forefinger.'

I considered a little and then said, 'On reflection, no. You are captain of this ship, and it is for you, therefore, to read the service. I will be present, of course.'

He looked a trifle dismayed, but said nothing more about it, and, after walking the deck with him for about half an hour, during which our talk was all about the 'Shark' and the incidents of the morning, what the crew thought of the duel and the like, I went below to my berth and lay down, feeling tired, hot, and again depressed. I was awakened out of a light sleep by the ringing of the first dinner bell. Having made ready for dinner I entered the cabin as the second bell sounded, and found the table prepared but no one present. I was standing at the foot of the companion ladder, trying to cool myself with the wind that breezed down of a fiery hue with the steadfast crimsoning of the westering sun, when Wilfrid came from his cabin. He was dressed as if for a ball—swallow-tail coat, patent leather boots, plenty of white shirt sparkling with diamond studs, and so forth. Indeed it was easily seen that he had attired himself with a most fastidious hand, as though on a sudden there had broken out in him a craze of dandyism. I was much astonished and stared at him. There had never been any ceremony amongst us; in point of meals we had made a sort of picnic of this marine ramble, and dined regardless of attire. Indeed, in this direction Wilfrid had always shown a singular negligence, often in cold weather sitting down in an old pilot coat, or taking his place during the hot days in white linen coat and small-clothes or an airy camlet jacket.

'Why, Wilf,' said I, running my eye over him, 'you must give me ten minutes to keep you in countenance.'

'No, no,' he cried, 'you are very well. This is a festal day with me, a time to be dignified with as much ceremony as the modern tailor will permit. Heavens! how on great occasions one misses the magnificence of one's forefathers. I should like to dine to-day in the costume of a Raleigh, a doublet bestudded with precious gems, a short cloak of cloth of gold. Ha, ha! a plague on the French Revolution. 'Tis all broadcloth now. Where's Laura?' He asked the question with a sudden breaking away from the substance of his speech that startlingly accentuated the wild look his eyes had and the expression of countenance that was a sort of baffling smile in its way.

'I do not know,' I answered.

'Oh, she must dine with us,' he cried. 'I want company. I should like to crowd this table. Steward, call Miss Jennings' maid.'

The man stole aft and tapped on the cabin next to the room occupied by Lady Monson. Miss Jennings opened the door and looked out. Wilfrid saw her and instantly ran to her with his finger upon his lip. He took her by the hand and whispered. She was clearly as much amazed as I had been to behold him attired as though for a rout. There was a little whispered talk between them; she apparently did not wish to join us; then on a sudden consented and he led her to the table, holding her hand with an air of old-world ceremony that must have provoked a smile but for the concern and anxiety his looks caused me. We took our places, and he fell to acting the part of host, pressing us to eat, calling for champagne, talking as if to entertain us. He laughed often, but softly, in a low-pitched key, and one saw that there was a perpetual reference in his mind to the existence of his wife close at hand, but he never once mentioned her nor referred to the dead man whose proximity put an indescribable quality of ghastliness into his hectic manner, the crazy air of conviviality that flushed, as with a glow of fever, his speech, and carriage, and behaviour of high breeding. Not a syllable concerning the events of the morning, the object of our excursion, its achievement, the change of the yacht's course, escaped him. He drank freely, but without any other result than throwing a little colour upon his high cheek-bones and rendering yet more puzzling the conflicting expressions which filled with wildness his large, protruding, near-sighted gaze at one or the other of us. I saw too clearly how it was with the poor fellow to feel shocked. Miss Laura's tact served her well in the replies she made to him, in the interest with which she seemed to listen to his conversation, in her well-feigned ignorance of there being anything unusual in his apparel or manner. But it failed her in her efforts to conceal her deep-seated apprehension, that stole like a shadow into her face when she looked downwards in some interval of silence that enabled her to think, or when her eyes met mine.

After dinner my cousin fetched his pipe and asked me to join him on deck. I took advantage of his absence to say swiftly to Miss Laura, 'We must not forget that Lady Monson is on board. Upon my word, I believe you are right in your suggestion this afternoon that Wilfrid has forgotten all about it, or surely he would have made some reference to her dining.'

'I'll take care that she is looked after, Mr. Monson,' she answered. 'I purposely abstained from mentioning her name at dinner. I am certain, by the expression in his face, that he would have been irritated by the lightest allusion to her, and unnatural as his mood is after such a morning as we have passed through,' here she glanced in the direction of the cabin where the Colonel's body lay, 'I would rather see him as he is than sullen, scowling, silent, eating up his heart.'

He returned with his pipe at that moment, and we were about to proceed on deck when he stopped and said to his sister-in-law, 'Come along, Laura, my love.'

'I have a slight headache, Wilfrid, and I have to see that my cabin is prepared.'

I thought this answer would start him into questioning her, but he looked as if he did not gather the meaning of it. 'Pooh, pooh,' he cried, 'there are two stewards and a maid to see to your cabin for you. If they don't suffice we'll have Muffin aft; that arthritic son of a greengrocer whose genius as a valet will scarcely be the worse for the tar that stains his hands. Muffin for one night only!' He delivered one of his short roars of laughter and slapped his leg.

By Jupiter! thought I, Lady Monson will hear *that* and take it as an expression of his delight at her presence on board! Does she know, I wondered, that her colonel lies dead? But I had found no opportunity of inquiring.

'Come along, Laura,' continued Wilfrid; 'I'll roll you up as pretty a cigarette as was ever smoked by a South American belle.'

She shook her head, forcing a smile.

'Perhaps Miss Jennings will join us later,' said I, distrustful of his temper, and passing my hand through his arm, I got him on deck.

'Laura is a sweet little woman,' said he, pausing just outside the hatch to hammer at a tinder-box.

'Ay, sweet, pretty, and good,' said I.

'You're in love with her, I think, Charles.'

'My dear Wilf, let us talk of this beautiful night,' I exclaimed.

'Why of a beautiful night in preference to a beautiful woman?' cried he.

But I was determined to end this, so I called to a figure standing to leeward of the main boom, 'Is that you, Finn?'

'No, it's me,' answered Crimp's surly note; 'the capt'n's a-laying down, but he's guv orders to be aroused at four bells.'

'Why?' inquired Wilfrid.

Crimp probably supposed the question put to me, for which I was thankful. 'He may mistrust the weather, perhaps,' I answered softly, that old Jacob might not hear. 'Yet the sky has a wonderfully settled look too. Let's go right aft, shall we, Wilf? The downdraught here is emptying my pipe.'

We strolled together to the grating abaft the wheel and seated ourselves. I cannot tell how much it affected me to find him so easily thrown off the line of his thoughts. It had been dark some time, for in those parallels night treads on the skirts of the glory which the departing sun trails down the western slope of the sea. There would be no moon sooner than ten o'clock or thereabouts, and it was now a little after eight—for my cousin's strange humour had made a much longer sitting than usual of the dinner. There was a refreshing sound of rushing wind in the star-laden dusk, a noise as of the sweeping of countless pinions, with a smooth hissing penetrating from the cutwater that made one think of the shearing of a skater over ice. The cabin lamps glowing into the skylight shed a yellow, satin-like sheen upon the foot of the mainsail, the cloths of which soared the paler for that lustre till the head of the gaff topsail looked like the brow of some height of vapour dissolving against the stars. We sat on a line with the side of the deck on which he had shot Colonel Hope-Kennedy. The gloom worked the memory of the incident in me into a phantasm, and I remember a little shiver creeping over me at the vision of that tall, noble figure with face upturned to heaven a moment or two as though he watched the flight of his spirit, then falling dead with the countenance of a man in easy slumber. But Wilfrid had not a word to say about it. I could not reconcile his extraordinary silence with his attire and manner, which at all events indicated the recollection of the duel as strong in him. He chattered volubly and intelligently, without any of his customary breakings away from his train of thought; but not of his wife, nor of the Colonel, nor of his infant, nor of this ocean chase that was now ended so far as the fugitives were concerned. He talked of his estate; how he intended to build a wing to his house that should contain a banqueting room, how he proposed to convert some acres of his land into a market garden, and so on and so on. His face showed pale in the starlight; his evening costume gave him an unusual look to my eye; though he talked carelessly on twenty matters of small interest, I could yet detect an undue energy in the tone of his voice, comparatively subdued as it was, and in his vehement manner of smoking, puffing out great clouds rapidly and filling the bowl afresh with hasty fingers. It would have vastly eased my mind had he made some reference to the morning. You felt as if the memory of it must be working in him like some deadly swift pulse, and I confess I could have shrunk from him at moments when I thought of the character of the source whence he drew the strength that enabled him to mask himself with what might well have passed for a mere company face.

When three bells, half-past nine, were struck, I made a move as though to go below.

'Going to turn in?' he asked.

'It has been a long, tiring day,' said I evasively.

'A grand day,' he exclaimed; 'the one stirring, memorable day of our voyage. Come, I will follow you, and we will pledge it in a bumper before parting.'

We entered the cabin; it was deserted. Wilfrid asked where Miss Laura was, and the steward replied that he believed she was gone to bed.

'She should be with us, Charles,' cried my cousin, with a light of excitement in his eyes, his face flushed, though above it had looked marble parently gazing into the obscurity astern where the Colonel's body was sinking and where the white wake of the yacht was glittering like a dusty summer highway running ivory-like through a dark land on a moonlit night. I watched her with anxiety, but without daring to approach her. The sailors unhitched the lanterns and took them forward along with the grating.

I said to Finn: 'I hope she does not mean to throw herself overboard.'

His head wagged in the moonlight. 'Sir,' he answered, 'the likes of her nature ain't quick to kill themselves. If she were the wife of the gent that's gone, I'd see to it. But *she'll* not hurt herself.'

Nevertheless, I kept my eye upon her. The awning was off the deck; the planks ran white as the foam alongside under the moon that was now brilliant, and all objects showed sharp upon that ground, whilst the flitting of the ebony shadows to the heave of the deck was like a crawling of spectral life. I spied the fellow at the glistening wheel turn his head repeatedly towards the woman abaft him, as though troubled by that wrapped, veiled, kneeling presence. Finn's rough, off-hand indifference could not reassure me. The fear of death, all horror induced by the cold, moonlit, desolate, weltering waters upon which her eyes were fixed might languish in the heat of some sudden craze of remorse, of grief, of despair. There were shapes of eddying froth striking out upon the dark liquid movement at which she was gazing—dim, scarce definable configurations of the sea-glow which to her sight might take the form of the man whose remains had just sped from the yacht's side; and God knows what sudden beckoning, what swift, endearing, caressing gesture to her to follow him she might witness in the apparition, real, sweet, alluring as in life to the gaze of her tragic eyes, which in imagination I could see glowing against the moon. It was with a deep sigh of relief that, after I had stood watching her at least ten minutes in the shadow of the gangway, I observed her dismount from the grating and walk to the companion, down which she seemed to melt away as ghostly in her coming as in her going. Twenty minutes later I followed her, found the cabin empty, and went straight to bed.

END OF THE SECOND VOLUME

*Spottiswoode & Co. Printers, New-street Square, London.*

www.ingramcontent.com/pod-product-compliance
Lightning Source LLC
Chambersburg PA
CBHW021048030726
47496CB00006B/1735